FUN學
美國各學科初級課本
新生入門英語閱讀 二版

1

AMERiCAN
SCHOOL
TEXTBOOK

Reading Key BASIC

如何下載 MP3 音檔

❶ **寂天雲 APP 聆聽：** 掃描書上 QR Code 下載「寂天雲 – 英日語學習隨身聽」APP。加入會員後，用 APP 內建掃描器再次掃描書上 QR Code，即可使用 APP 聆聽音檔。

❷ **官網下載音檔：** 請上「寂天閱讀網」（www.icosmos.com.tw），註冊會員／登入後，搜尋本書，進入本書頁面，點選「MP3 下載」下載音檔，存於電腦等其他播放器聆聽使用。

The Best Preparation for Building Academic Reading Skills and Vocabulary

The Reading Key series is designed to help students to understand American school textbooks and to develop background knowledge in a wide variety of academic topics. This series also provides learners with the opportunity to enhance their reading comprehension skills and vocabulary.

- o **Reading Key** <**Basic 1–4**> is a four-book series designed for beginning learners.

- o **Reading Key** <**Volume 1–3**> is a three-book series designed for beginner to intermediate learners.

- o **Reading Key** <**Volume 4–6**> is a three-book series designed for intermediate to high-intermediate learners.

- o **Reading Key** <**Volume 7–9**> is a three-book series designed for high-intermediate learners.

Features

- A wide variety of topics that cover American school subjects
- Intensive practice for reading skill development
- Building vocabulary through school subjects and themed texts
- Graphic organizers for each passage
- Captivating pictures and illustrations related to the topics

Table of Contents

Component

• Workbook

Syllabus Vol. 1

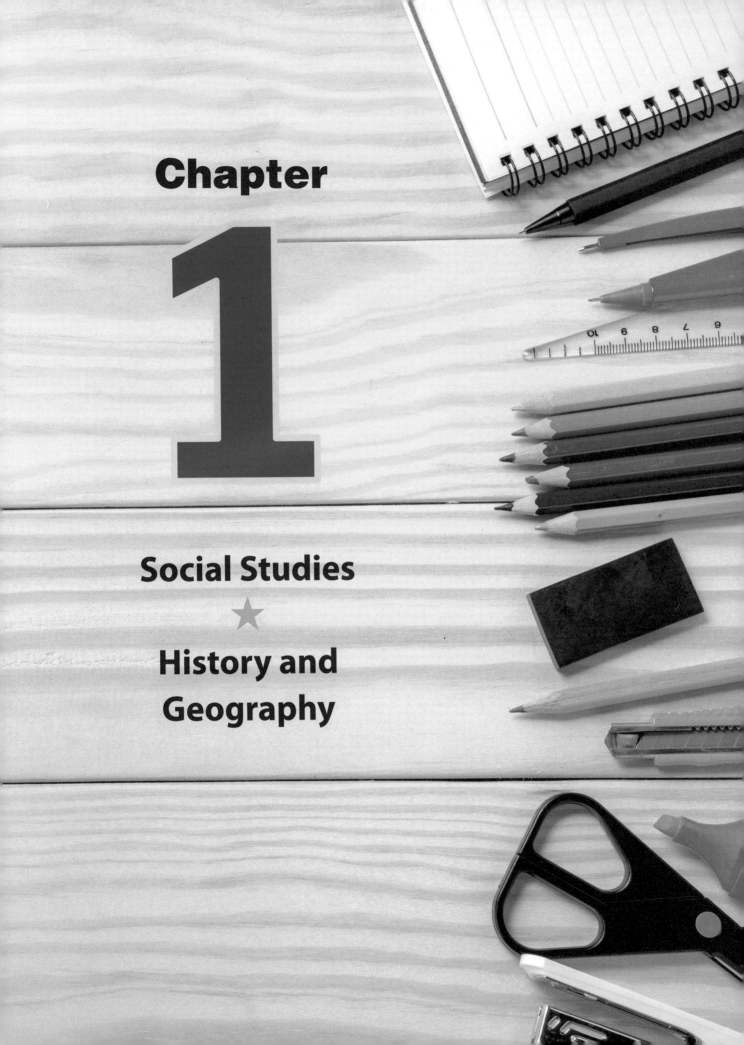

Chapter

1

Social Studies

★

History and
Geography

Unit 01

Seasons and Weather

Reading Focus

- What are the four seasons?
- What are some kinds of weather?
- How does weather change?

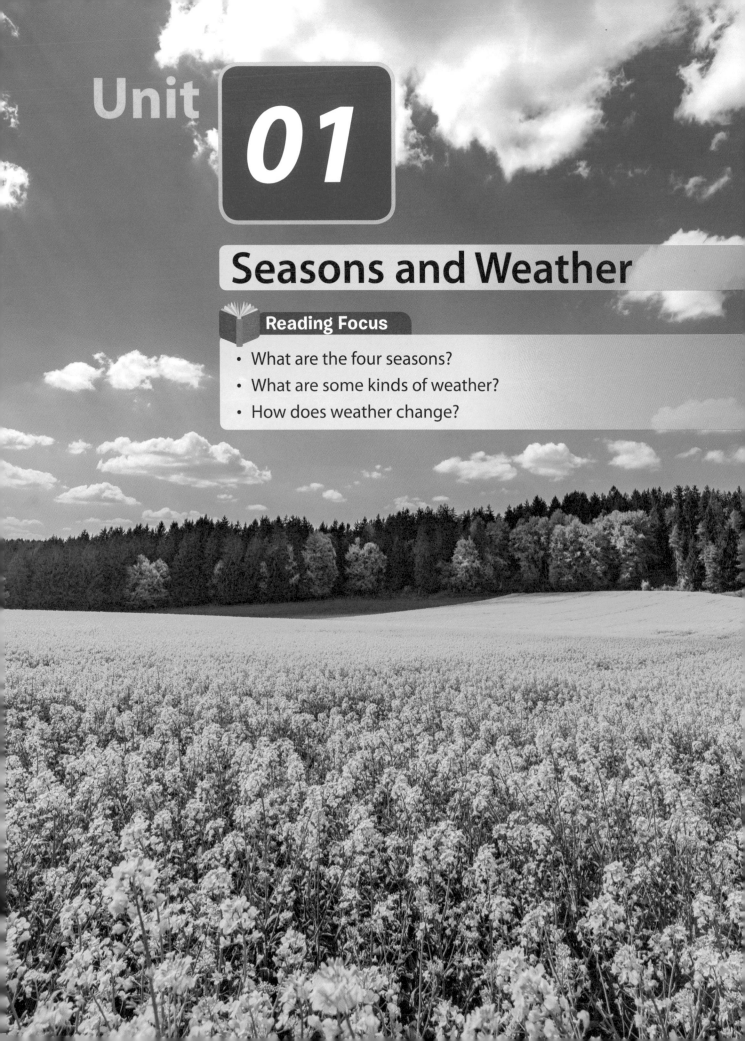

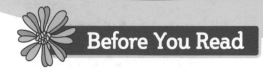 **Before You Read**

 01

Key Words

sunny

Weather

cloudy

rainy

snowy

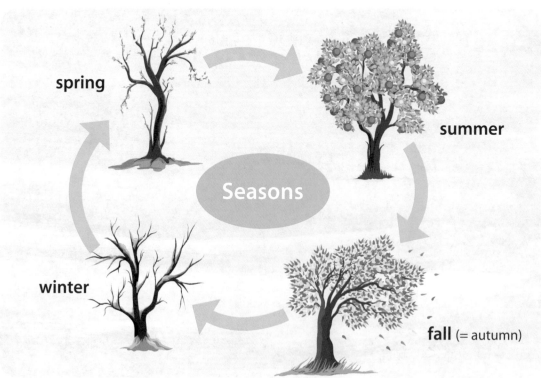

spring

Seasons

summer

winter

fall (= autumn)

Power Verbs

rain
It is **raining**.

snow
It is **snowing**.

bloom
Flowers **bloom**.

change
Leaves **change** colors.

Word Families: Comparative and Superlative

hot < hotter < hottest

cold < colder < coldest

warm < warmer < warmest

cool < cooler < coolest

Seasons and Weather

Look outside.
Is it sunny? Is it cloudy?

Weather changes from day to day.
It can be sunny.
It can be cloudy.
It can be rainy or snowy.

Weather changes from season to season, too.
A year has four seasons.
They are spring, summer, fall, and winter.

Spring is warm.
Flowers begin to bloom in spring.

Summer comes after spring.
Summer is very hot and sunny.
It is the warmest season.

▲ Flowers bloom in spring.

▲ Summer is very sunny.

Seasons Change

Spring is warm.

Summer is hot.

Fall is cool.

Winter is cold.

Fall comes after summer.
Fall is cooler than summer.
Leaves change colors in fall.

Winter comes after fall.
Winter is very cold and snowy.
It is the coldest season.

▲ Leaves change colors in fall.

▲ Winter can be snowy.

Check Understanding

1 **Which season does each picture show?**

a

b

_____   _____

2 **Which season is the coldest?**

a summer   b fall   c winter

3 **What happens to trees in fall?**

a Flowers bloom.   b Leaves change colors.
c Leaves turn green.

4 **Summer can be _____.**

a hot   b cool   c snowy

• **Answer the questions below.**

1 What are the four seasons?
⇨ They are _____, _____, _____, and _____.

2 Which season comes after winter?
⇨ _____ comes after winter.

A **Look, Read, and Write.**
Look at the pictures. Write the correct words.

> rainy   bloom   cloudy   change colors

1 ▸ The weather can be _____.

2 ▸ The weather can be _____.

3 ▸ Flowers _____ in spring.

4 ▸ Leaves _____ in fall.

B **Warmer or Warmest?**
Draw a circle around the right words and then write the words.

1 Spring is _____ than winter.
　　　cooler　warmer

2 Summer is the _____ season.
　　　coolest　warmest

3 Fall is _____ than summer.
　　　cooler　warmer

4 Winter is the _____ season.
　　　coldest　warmest

Unit 02

Our Land and Water

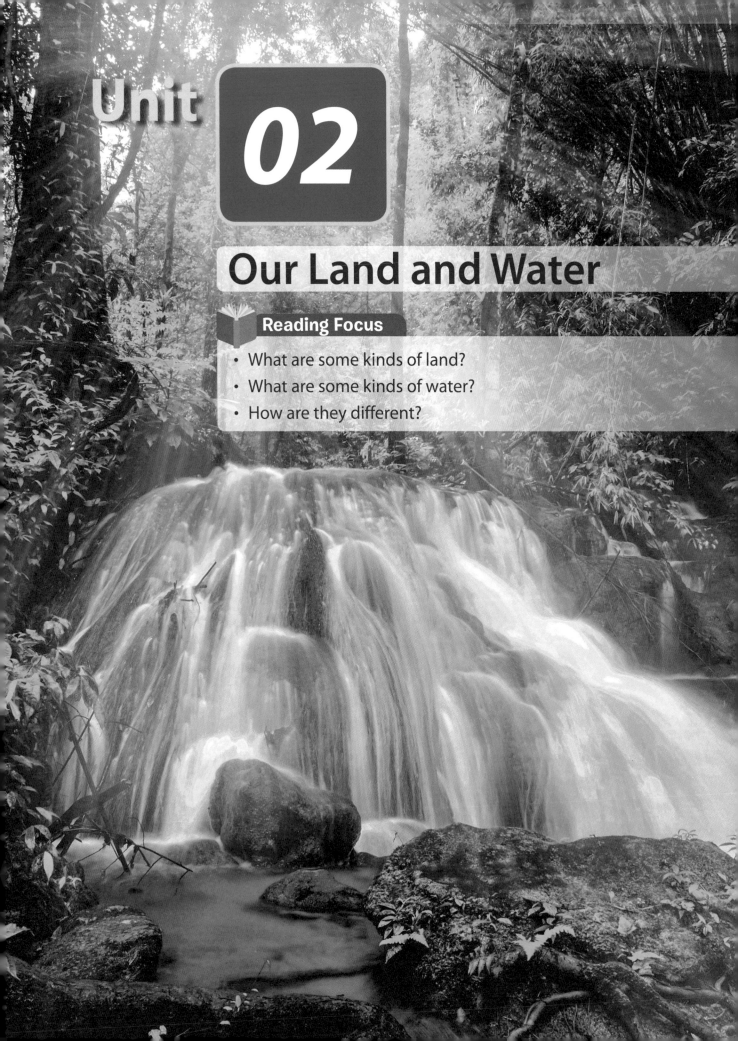

Reading Focus

- What are some kinds of land?
- What are some kinds of water?
- How are they different?

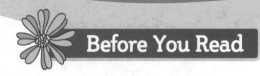

Before You Read

03

Key Words

mountain

hill

valley

Kinds of Land

plain

desert

island

Kinds of Water

ocean

lake

river

Power Verbs

be made up of
Earth **is made up of** land and water.

be surrounded by
An island **is surrounded by** water.

cover
Oceans **cover** much of our Earth.

flow into
Rivers **flow into** oceans.

Word Families: The Adjectives for Land

mountain

high < higher

hill

low < lower

plain

flat

valley

narrow

desert

dry

Our Land and Water

Earth is made up of land and water.
This is a picture of Earth.
Can you tell which part is land?
Which part is water?

▲ Earth is made up of land and water.

Earth has different kinds of land.

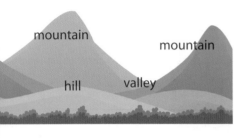

A mountain is the highest form of land.
A hill is lower than a mountain.
A valley is the low land between mountains.
A valley is usually narrow.

Some land is flat.
Flat land is called a plain.
A plain is good for farming.

▲ A plain is good for farming.

A desert is a dry land.
A desert has very little rain.
An island is surrounded by water.

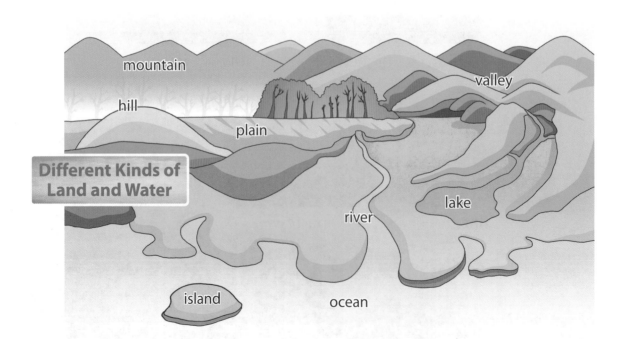

Different Kinds of Land and Water

Earth has different kinds of water.

An ocean is the largest body of water.
Oceans cover much of our Earth.

A lake is a large body of water.
It is surrounded by land.

A river is a long body of water.
It flows into an ocean.

▲ Oceans cover much of our Earth.

▲ A river flows into an ocean.

Check Understanding

1 **Which land does each picture show?**

 a

 b

_____   _____

2 **What is the lowest form of land?**
   a a hill   b a plain   c a mountain

3 **What is the low land between mountains?**
   a a valley   b a plain   c a hill

4 **A _____ is surrounded by land.**
   a lake   b river   c island

• **Answer the questions below.**

1 What are some different kinds of land?
⇨ _____, hills, _____, _____, deserts, and _____
are kinds of land.

2 What are some different kinds of water?
⇨ _____, _____, and _____ are kinds of water.

Vocabulary and Grammar Builder

A **Look, Read, and Write.**
Look at the pictures. Write the correct words.

narrow   farming   dry   lower

 **1** ▸ A hill is _____ than a mountain.

 **2** ▸ A valley is usually _____.

 **3** ▸ A desert is a _____ land.

 **4** ▸ A plain is good for _____.

B **Of or On?**
Draw a circle around the right words and then write the words.

1 Earth is made up _____ land and water.
of   on

2 An island is surrounded _____ water.
at   by

3 A river flows _____ an ocean.
into   onto

4 A valley is _____ two mountains.
under   between

Unit 03

Many Jobs

 Reading Focus

- What is a job?
- Why do people work?
- What are some jobs that people do?
- What are some jobs that volunteers do?

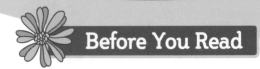

Key Words

waiter

Service Jobs

doctor

bus driver

deliveryman

Community Jobs

police officer

firefighter

mail carrier

Volunteers

help others

work for free

Power Verbs

work
He **works** hard.

earn
People **earn** money at work.

feed
I **feed** my dog.

water
I **water** plants.

serve
A waiter **serves** food.

Word Families: What They Do?

Jobs	What They Do

 **farmers** ➡ grow fruits and vegetables

 **doctors** ➡ help sick people

 **waiters** ➡ serve food at restaurants

 **firefighters** ➡ put out fires

Many Jobs

My name is John. This is my home.
I do lots of jobs to help at home.
I feed my dog. I water the plants.
I help my mom cook dinner.

What are your jobs at home?

A job is the work people do.
Most people have jobs to earn money.

There are many kinds of jobs.
Farmers grow fruits and vegetables.
Some workers work in factories.

Some people have service jobs.
A waiter serves food at a restaurant.
A doctor helps people who are sick.

Some people work for the community.
Firefighters put out dangerous fires.
Police officers work for the safety of the community.

▲ Some people work in factories.

▲ Some people work for the community.

Some workers are volunteers.
Volunteers work for free to help others.
Some volunteers serve food to homeless people.
Some volunteers work at hospitals.

All kinds of work are important.
What kind of work would you like to do?

▲ Volunteers help
others for free.

Check Understanding

1 Which job does each picture show?

a

b

_____   _____

2 Why do most people work?
   a to serve food   b to earn money   c to help sick people

3 What do volunteers do?
   a work in factories   b earn money   c help others

4 _____ work for the safety of the community.
   a Farmers   b Waiters   c Police officers

• **Answer the questions below.**

1 What are some jobs that people do at home?
   ⇨ Some people _____ their dogs and _____ their plants.

2 What are some jobs that volunteers do?
   ⇨ They _____ food to homeless people or work at _____ .

A **Look, Read, and Write.**
Look at the pictures. Write the correct words.

earn money   work for free   police officers   factories

1 ▸ Most people have jobs to _____.

2 ▸ _____ work for the community.

3 ▸ Volunteers _____ to help others.

4 ▸ Some workers work in _____.

B **What Do They Do?**
Draw a circle around the right words and then write the words.

1   Farmers _____ fruits and vegetables.
     grow   cook

2   Waiters _____ at restaurants.
     serve food   work for free

3   Doctors _____ people who are sick.
     feed   help

4   Firefighters _____ dangerous fires.
     put out   put on

04

Transportation

 Reading Focus

- What is transportation?
- Why do people use transportation?
- What kinds of transportation are there?

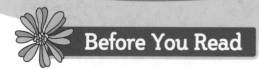 Before You Read

07

Key Words

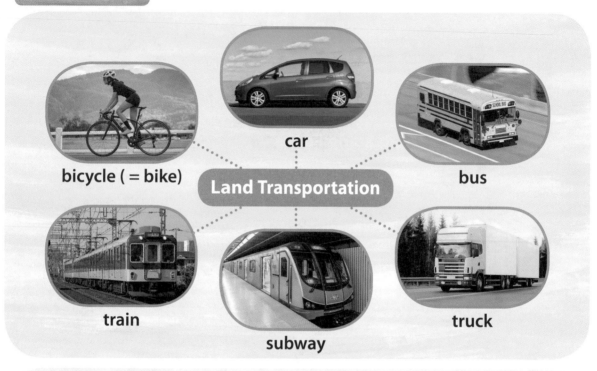

bicycle (= bike)

car

bus

Land Transportation

train

subway

truck

Air Transportation

airplane

helicopter

jet

Water Transportation

ship

ferry

cargo ship

Power Verbs

ride
She **rides** her bike.

take
They **take** the school bus.

carry
Trains **carry** many things at one time.

transport
Ferries **transport** people.

Word Families

a bus driver ➡ drives a bus

a delivery truck ➡ delivers things

an airplane ➡ flies in the air

a ship ➡ moves on the water

Transportation

Jenny is a student.
She rides her bike to school.
Sometimes she takes the school bus, too.

▲ Jenny rides her bike to school.

The bike and the school bus are her transportation.
Transportation moves people or things from one place to another.

What kinds of transportation do you use?

Some people drive their cars to work.
Some people take the subway to work.
Some people take buses to work.

▲ Some people take the subway to work.

Some kinds of transportation move a lot of things at one time.
A delivery truck delivers things to people.
A tanker truck carries oil and gas.
A train can also carry a lot of things at one time.

▲ tanker truck

Different Kinds of Transportation

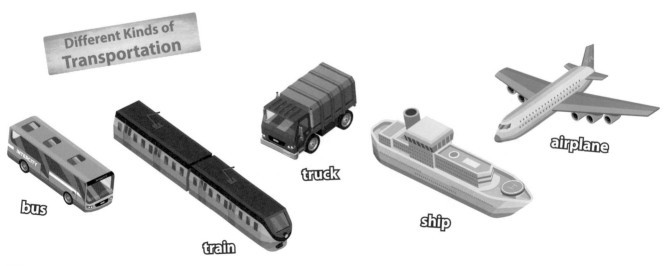

bus

train

truck

ship

airplane

Airplanes and helicopters move in the air.
Airplanes can fly around the world to
transport people and goods.

People also travel on the water.
Many ships and ferries transport people
and goods.

▲ Airplanes move in the air.

▲ Ships move on the water.

Check Understanding

1   Which type of transportation does each picture show?

a

b

_____   _____

2   What moves people or things from one place to another?
a food   b transportation   c shopping mall

3   What do tanker trucks carry?
a oil and gas   b people   c the mail

4   A _____ moves in the air.
a ferry   b helicopter   c delivery truck

• **Answer the questions below.**

1 Why do people use transportation?
   ⇨ People use transportation to _____ from one place to _____.

2 What kinds of transportation move on the water?
   ⇨ _____ and _____ move on the water.

A **Look, Read, and Write.**
Look at the pictures. Write the correct words.

| carry | transportation | buses | transport |

1  ▸ A car is one type of _____.

2  ▸ Trucks _____ many things at one time.

3  ▸ Some people take _____ to work.

4  ▸ Ferries _____ people or goods.

B **Take or Takes?**
Draw a circle around the right words and then write the words.

1   Jenny _____ her bike to school.
　　　　　ride   rides

2   Some people _____ the subway to work.
　　　　　　take   takes

3   A helicopter _____ in the sky.
　　　　　fly   flies

4   A delivery truck _____ things to people.
　　　　　deliver   delivers

A Look at the pictures. Write the correct words.

bloom   firefighters   carries   surrounded

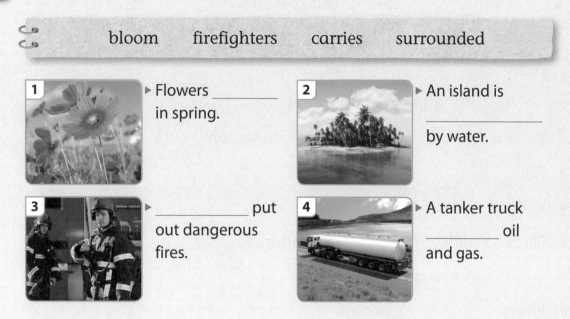

1 ▶ Flowers _____ in spring.

2 ▶ An island is _____ by water.

3 ▶ _____ put out dangerous fires.

4 ▶ A tanker truck _____ oil and gas.

B Draw a circle around the right words and then write the words.

summer   fall

1   Fall comes _____ summer.
　　　　before   after

2   A waiter _____ food at a restaurant.
　　　　serve   serves

3   A valley is the _____ between mountains.
　　　　high land   low land

4   A _____ moves on the water.
　　jet   ship

C Complete the sentences with the words below.

warmer	change colors	winter	season
flow into	flat land	made up of	kinds of

1 Leaves _____ in fall.

2 _____ comes before spring.

3 Weather changes from _____ to season.

4 Fall is _____ than winter.

5 Earth is _____ land and water.

6 Earth has different _____ land.

7 _____ is called a plain.

8 Rivers _____ oceans.

D Complete the sentences with the words below.

serve	in the air	job	transportation
drive	work for	earn	rides

1 A _____ is the work people do.

2 Most people have jobs to _____ money.

3 Some people _____ the community.

4 Some volunteers _____ food to homeless people.

5 _____ moves people or things from one place to another.

6 Jenny _____ her bike to school.

7 Some people _____ their cars to work.

8 Airplanes and helicopters move _____.

Chapter

2

Science

Unit 05

A World of Plants

Reading Focus

- What are some kinds of plants?
- What are some parts of a plant?
- What plant parts do we eat?

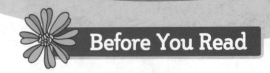

 09

Key Words

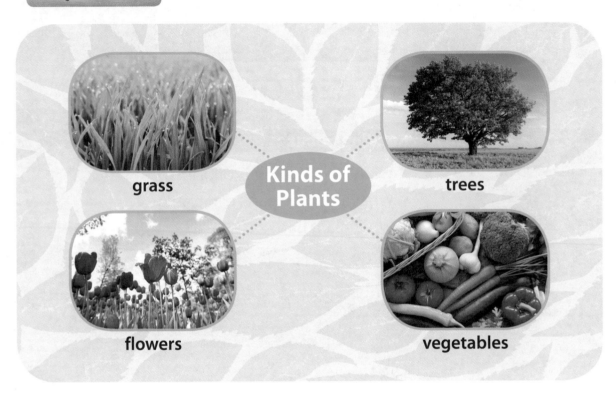

grass

Kinds of Plants

trees

flowers

vegetables

The Parts of a Plant

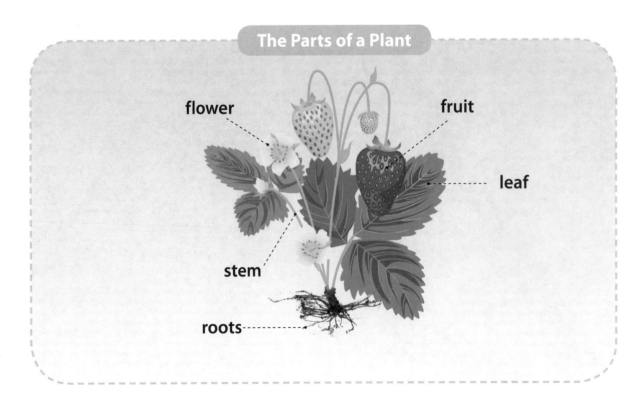

flower

fruit

leaf

stem

roots

Power Verbs

grow
I **grow** plants.

live
Plants **live** in many places.

hold
The fruits **hold** seeds.

Word Families: The Parts of Plants

roots
Some **roots** are **thick**.
Some **roots** are **thin**.

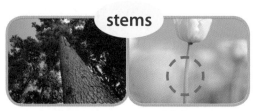
stems
Some **stems** are **thick**.
Some **stems** are **thin**.

leaves
Some **leaves** are **big**.
Some **leaves** are **little**.

fruits
Some plants **have** fruits.
Some plants **do not have** fruits.

seeds
Some **seeds** are **big**.
Some **seeds** are **small**.

A World of Plants

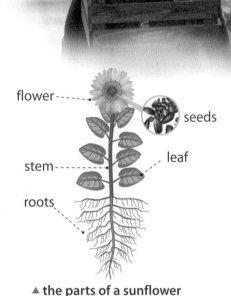

I grow many plants in my garden.

I am Scott. And this is my garden.
I grow many plants here.

There are many different kinds of plants.
Plants can be big or small.
Grass, vegetables, and trees are all plants.

Plants have different parts.
Most plants have roots, stems, and leaves.
Many plants have flowers, too.
The flowers make fruits.
The fruits hold seeds.

flower

seeds

stem

leaf

roots

▲ the parts of a sunflower

We can eat many plant parts.

We eat roots.
Radishes, onions, and carrots are the roots of plants.
We eat stems.
Celery is the stem of a plant.

▲ Celery is a stem.

We eat leaves, such as lettuce and cabbage.
We eat flowers, such as broccoli and cauliflower.

▲ Radishes and carrots are roots.

▲ Broccoli and cauliflower are flowers.

We eat the fruits of many plants, too.
Apples, pears, and strawberries are fruits we eat.

Sometimes we eat the seeds of plants, too.
Corn, rice, and peanuts are all the seeds of plants.

▲ We eat the fruits of many plants.

▲ Sometimes we eat the seeds of plants.

Check Understanding

1 **Which plant part does each picture show?**

a

b

c

These are both _____.

These are both _____.

These are both _____.

2 **What do flowers make?**
   a stems   b leaves   c fruits

3 **Which plant flowers do we eat?**
   a corn   b broccoli   c carrots

4 **We eat the _____ of corn and rice plants.**
   a seeds   b stems   c leaves

• **Answer the questions below.**

1 What parts do most plants have?
   ⇨ Most plants have _____, _____, and _____.

2 What are some roots that people eat?
   ⇨ People eat _____, _____, and _____.

Vocabulary and Grammar Builder

A **Look, Read, and Write.**
Look at the pictures. Write the correct words.

grow	hold	vegetables	seeds

1  ► _____ are kinds of plants.

2 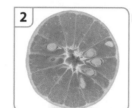 ► The fruits _____ seeds.

3  ► People _____ different kinds of plants.

4  ► Sometimes we eat the _____ of plants.

B **One or More?**
Draw a circle around the right words and then write the words.

1 a _____
leaf   leaves

 many _____
leaf   leaves

2 A _____ is the root of a plant.
radish   radishes

3 _____ are delicious seeds.
A corn   Corns

4  _____ are fruits we eat.
A strawberry   Strawberries

Unit 06

A World of Animals

Reading Focus

- What are some kinds of animals?
- Where do these animals live?
- What do animals need to live?

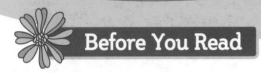

Before You Read

Key Words

Land Animals

squirrel   deer   giraffe

snake   lizard

polar bear   penguin

Water Animals

goldfish

shark

whale

dolphin

forest

grassland

desert

Places to Live

the North Pole

the South Pole

ocean

Power Verbs

need
Animals **need** food and water.

breathe
Land animals **breathe** air.

Word Families

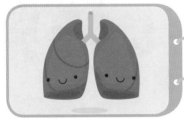

lungs
Lungs help animals breathe.

gills
Gills help fish breathe.

tiny
Ants are **tiny**.

huge
Elephants are **huge**.

favorite
My **favorite** animals are dogs.

like
I **like** dogs.

A World of Animals

What's your favorite animal?
Do you like dogs? Do you like cats?

There are many different kinds of animals.
Some animals are tiny like ants.
Some animals are huge like elephants.

Animals need food and water to live.
Some animals eat plants.
Some animals eat other animals.

Animals need air, too.
Lungs help animals breathe air.
Gills help fish breathe in water.

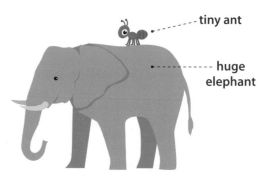

tiny ant

huge elephant

All animals need places to live, too.
Animals live in different places.

Many animals live in forests.
Bears, squirrels, and deer live in forests.

Other animals live in grasslands.
Giraffes, elephants, and lions live in grasslands.

Some animals, like snakes and lizards, live in deserts.

grassland

forest

desert

▲ Animals live in different places.

A few animals live in very cold places.
Polar bears live at the North Pole.
Penguins live at the South Pole.

And fish live in water.
Sharks, whales, and dolphins live in the ocean.

▲ A few animals live
  in very cold places.

▲ Fish live in water.

Check Understanding

1 What place does each picture show?

a

b

_____

_____

2 What is a huge animal?

a an elephant   b an ant   c a dog

3 What lives in a forest?

a a penguin   b a goldfish   c a deer

4 Animals use _____ to breathe air.

a gills   b lungs   c heart

• **Answer the questions below.**

1 Which animals live in grasslands?

⇨ _____, _____, and lions live in grasslands.

2 Where do penguins live?

⇨ Penguins live at the _____ _____.

A **Look, Read, and Write.**
Look at the pictures. Write the correct words.

> huge   tiny   breathe   need

1  ▶ Lungs help animals _____ air.

2 ▶ Animals _____ food and water to live.

3  ▶ Elephants are _____ animals.

4  ▶ Ants are _____.

B **Where Do They Live?**
Draw a circle around the right words and then write the words.

1 Squirrels live in _____.
        forest   grassland

2 Lizards live in _____.
        ocean   desert

3 Dolphins live in the _____.
        ocean   desert

4 Polar bears live at the _____.
        South Pole   North Pole

Unit 07

A World of Insects

Reading Focus

- What are some insects?
- How are insects alike?
- How many body parts does an insect have?

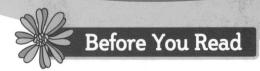

Before You Read

13

Key Words

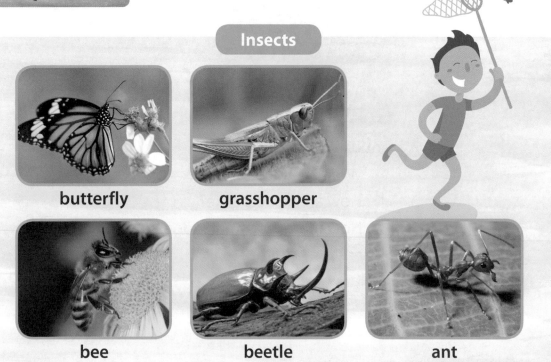

Insects

butterfly

grasshopper

bee

beetle

ant

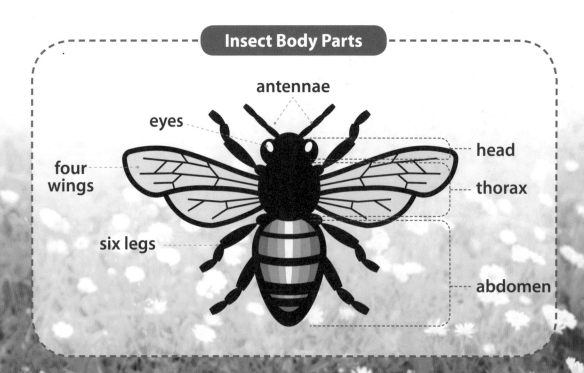

Insect Body Parts

antennae

eyes

four wings

six legs

head

thorax

abdomen

50

Power Verbs

come in
Insects **come in** many shapes.

take a look
Take a look at the ants.

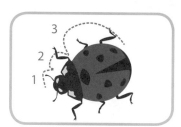

be divided into
Insects **are divided into** three parts.

touch
Insects **touch** with their antennae.

Word Families: Bees and Ants

Kinds of Bees

queen bee   male bee   **female bee** = worker bee

Kinds of Ants

queen ant   male ant   worker ant

A World of Insects

Look at the pictures.
Can you name each of them?

| ant | honeybee | butterfly | beetle |

They are all insects.

Insects come in many colors, shapes, and sizes.
But every insect has three body parts: a head, thorax, and abdomen.
And insects all have six legs.
Some insects have wings and can fly. Some have no wings.

Ants and bees are both insects.
Take a look at them.

How many legs do they have?
They all have six legs, right?

Their bodies are divided into
three parts.

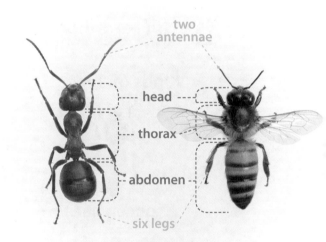

▲ Insects have
three body parts.

Their eyes and antennae are on their heads.
The antennae help insects touch and smell.

Their legs are on their thoraxes.

Bees have wings there, too. So bees can fly.

But most ants do not have wings.

Only queen ants and male ants have wings.

The abdomen is the largest part of most insects.

wing

▲ A bee has wings on its thorax.

▲ The abdomen is the largest part of most insects.

Check Understanding

1 **Which body part does each picture show?**

a

b

_____   _____

2 **How many legs do insects have?**
   a three   b four   c six

3 **Where are an insect's antennae?**
   a on its head   b on its thorax   c on its abdomen

4 **Bees have _____ so they can fly.**
   a antennae   b insects   c wings

• **Answer the questions below.**

1 How do insects use their antennae?
   ⇨ They use their antennae to _____ and _____.

2 What is the largest part of most insects?
   ⇨ The largest part of most insects is the _____.

Vocabulary and Grammar Builder

A **Look, Read, and Write.**
Look at the pictures. Write the correct words.

come in   bees   head   body parts

1  ▶ An insect's eyes are on its _____.

2  ▶ Insects _____ many shapes and sizes.

3 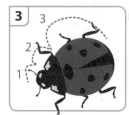 ▶ All insects have three _____.

4  ▶ _____ have wings.

B **What Body Parts?**
Draw a circle around the right words and then write the words.

1 All insects have a head, _____, and abdomen.
                        thorax   wings

2 All insects have six _____.
                    wings   legs

3 Insects use their _____ to smell.
                 head   antennae

4 Insects with _____ can fly.
            wings   abdomens

Unit

08

What Are the Five Senses?

Reading Focus

- What are the five senses?
- What body parts do you use for each sense?
- How do you use your senses?

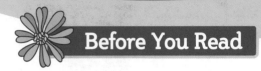

Before You Read

15

Key Words

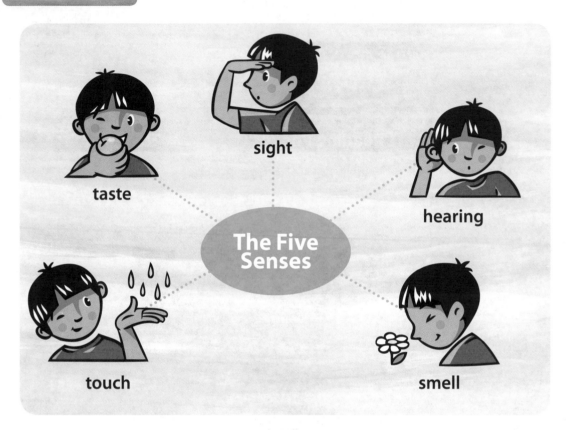

taste

sight

hearing

The Five Senses

touch

smell

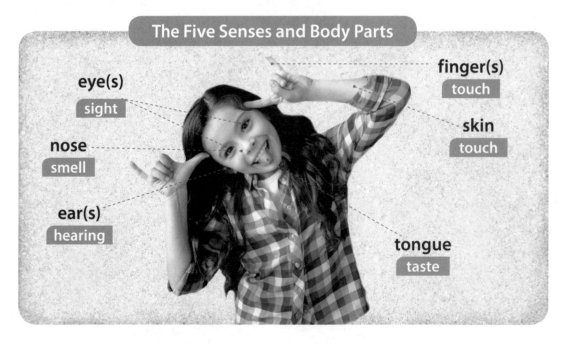

The Five Senses and Body Parts

eye(s)
sight

nose
smell

ear(s)
hearing

finger(s)
touch

skin
touch

tongue
taste

Power Verbs

see
She can **see** the flower.

hear
He can **hear** the music.

smell
It **smells** good.

taste
This cake **tastes** sweet.

touch
Don't **touch** that hot stove.

Word Families: Senses

tastes

- bitter
- sour
- salty
- sweet

feelings

| smooth | rough |
| hot | cold |

sight

- colorful
- black and white

sounds

| loud | noisy |
| soft | quiet |

smell

- fragrant
- smelly

What Are the Five Senses?

Mary hears her alarm clock ringing in the morning.
She wakes up and looks around her room.
She smells breakfast.
It smells good.
She gets up and eats her breakfast.
It tastes good.

▲ wake up

▲ get up

We use our senses every day.
People have five senses.
They are sight, hearing, smell, taste, and touch.

You use different body parts for different senses.

You use your eyes to see.
When you see, you know how things look.

▲ We use different body parts for different senses.

You use your ears to hear.
When you hear, you take in sound and understand it.

You use your nose to smell.
Smell tells you how things smell.

The Five Senses

sight   smell   hearing   taste   touch

You use your tongue to taste.

Taste tells you if food is sweet, sour, salty, or bitter.

Chocolate tastes sweet. Lemons taste sour.

▲ Chocolate tastes sweet.

You use your fingers and skin to feel.

Touch tells you if things are smooth, rough, hot, or cold.

A teddy bear feels smooth. A stove feels hot.

▲ A teddy bear feels smooth.

Check Understanding

1 Which sense does each picture show?

a

She is using her sense of _____ .

b

They are using their senses of _____ and hearing.

2 How many senses do people have?

a three   b five   c ten

3 Which sense do we use when we see something?

a hearing   b taste   c sight

4 You use your _____ to feel things.

a nose   b fingers   c eyes

• **Answer the questions below.**

1 What are the five senses?

⇨ They are _____, _____, _____, _____, and _____ .

2 What are some tastes for foods?

⇨ They are _____, _____, _____, and _____ .

Vocabulary and Grammar Builder

A **Look, Read, and Write.**
Look at the pictures. Write the correct words.

| smooth | wakes up | take in | sour |

 **1**
▶ Mary _____ early in the morning.

 **2**
▶ Lemon tastes _____.

 **3**
▶ When you hear, you _____ sound.

 **4**
▶ A teddy bear feels _____.

B **One or More?**
Draw a circle around the right words and then write the words.

1 The eyes _____ things.
see   sees

2 The tongue _____ foods.
taste   tastes

3 The ears _____ sounds.
hear   hears

4 The fingers _____ different things.
feel   feels

A Look at the pictures. Write the correct words.

tastes　　gills　　roots　　body parts

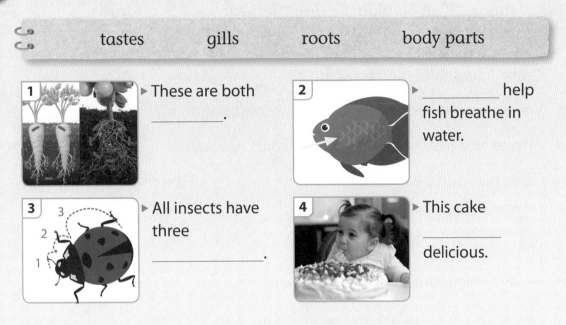

1 These are both _____.

2 _____ help fish breathe in water.

3 All insects have three _____.

4 This cake _____ delicious.

B Draw a circle around the right words and then write the words.

1 _____ are delicious fruits.
　　An orange　oranges

2 Penguins live at the _____.
　　　　　　　　　　South Pole　North Pole

3 All insects have a head, _____, and abdomen.
　　　　　　　　　　thorax　wings

4 This flower _____ good.
　　smell　smells

C Complete the sentences with the words below.

> lungs   plants   lettuce   fruits
> deserts   ocean   grasslands   seeds

1 Grass, vegetables, and trees are all _____.

2 We eat leaves, such as _____ and cabbage.

3 Apples and pears are _____ we eat.

4 Corn, rice, and peanuts are all the _____ of the plants.

5 _____ help animals breathe air.

6 Snakes and lizards live in _____.

7 Giraffes, elephants, and lions live in _____.

8 Sharks, whales, and dolphins live in the _____.

D Complete the sentences with the words below.

> antennas   insects   come in   thoraxes
> tongue   sight   see   touch

1 _____ have three body parts and six legs.

2 Insects _____ many colors, shapes, and sizes.

3 The _____ help insects touch and smell.

4 Insects' legs are on their _____ .

5 The five senses are _____, hearing, smell, taste, and touch.

6 When you _____, you know how things look.

7 You use your _____ to taste.

8 _____ tells you if things are smooth, rough, hot, or cold.

Chapter

3

Language

★

Mathematics

★

Visual Arts

★

Music

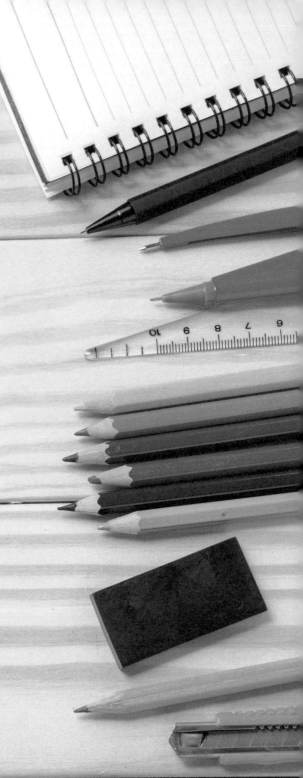

Unit 09

The Little Red Hen

Reading Focus

- Which animals lived on the little red hen's farm?
- What sounds do those animals make?
- Why did the little red hen eat the bread all by herself?

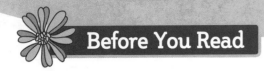

17

Key Words

Who Is in the Story?

hen

pig

duck

cat

Farm Crops

wheat

corn

rice

barley

Power Verbs

oink
Pigs oinked.

quack
Ducks quacked.

meow
Cats meowed.

cluck
Hens clucked.

Word Families: Past Tense

plant ⇨ planted

grow ⇨ grew

bake ⇨ baked

From planting to baking bread

harvest ⇨ harvested

grind ⇨ ground

cut⇨ cut

The Little Red Hen

Once upon a time, there was a little red hen.
She lived on a farm with a pig, a duck, and a cat.
She worked hard every day.
But the other animals never helped.

One day, the little red hen found some grains of wheat
in the garden.
"We can plant these seeds, and they will grow,"
thought the hen.
So she asked,
"Who will help me plant this wheat?"
"Not I," oinked the pig.
"Not I," quacked the duck.
"Not I," meowed the cat.
"Very well then. I will do it myself," clucked the little red hen.

During the summer,
the seeds of wheat grew.
Then, the wheat turned a golden color.
When it was ready to be harvested,
the little red hen asked,
"Who will help me cut the wheat?"
"Not I," oinked the pig.

"Not I," quacked the duck.
"Not I," meowed the cat.
"Very well then. I will do it myself," clucked the little red hen.

When she had cut the wheat, the little red hen asked,
"Who will help me grind this wheat into flour?"
"Not I," oinked the pig.
"Not I," quacked the duck.
"Not I," meowed the cat.
"Very well then. I will do it myself,"
clucked the little red hen.

When she had ground the wheat into flour,
the little red hen asked,
"Now who will help me bake the bread?"
"Not I," oinked the pig.
"Not I," quacked the duck.
"Not I," meowed the cat.
"Very well then. I will do it myself,"
clucked the little red hen.

Finally, the bread came out of the oven.
It looked and smelled delicious.

The little red hen asked,
"Now who will help me eat the bread?"
"I will," oinked the pig.
"I will," quacked the duck.
"I will," meowed the cat.
"Oh, no, you won't," said the little red hen.
"I planted the wheat all by myself.
I cut the wheat all by myself.
I ground the wheat grain into flour all by myself.
And I baked the bread all by myself.
Now, I will eat the bread—all by myself!"
And that is what she did.
The little red hen ate the bread all by herself.

1 **Which action does each picture show?**

The little red hen is
_____ the wheat.

The little red hen is
_____ the wheat.

2 **What sound does a hen make?**
a meow   b quack   c cluck

3 **How did the little red hen make the wheat into flour?**
a She planted it.   b She ground it.   c She baked it.

4 **The little red hen baked the bread in her _____.**
a farm   b garden   c oven

5 **What does "all by myself" mean?**
a alone (without help)   b together   c each other

6 **Match the animals and the sound that each animal makes.**

a Pigs   •   •   meow (meowed)
b Ducks •   •   oink (oinked)
c Cats   •   •   quack (quacked)
d Hens •   •   cluck (clucked)

• **Answer the questions below.**

1 Which animals lived on the little red hen's farm?
⇨ A _____, a _____, and a _____ lived on her farm.

2 Who ate the bread the little red hen baked?
⇨ The little red hen ate the bread _____ _____ _____.

A **Look, Read, and Write.**
Look at the pictures. Write the correct words.

| flour | harvested | planted | found |

 **1** ▸ She _____ some grains of wheat.

 **2** ▸ She _____ the wheat.

 **3** ▸ She _____ the seeds of wheat.

4 ▸ She used _____ to make the bread.

B **The Past Forms of Verbs**
Draw a circle around the past form of each verb and then write the verb.

1 The little red hen _____ the seeds. (plant)
plantted   planted

2 The little red hen _____ the wheat. (cut)
cut   cutted

3 The little red hen _____ the wheat into flour. (grind)
ground   grounded

4 The little red hen _____ the bread. (bake)
bakeed   baked

Unit 10

Numbers from 1 to 10

Reading Focus

- What are the numbers from 1 to 10?
- Which number comes after 1?
- What numbers are less than 5?

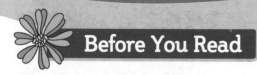

Key Words

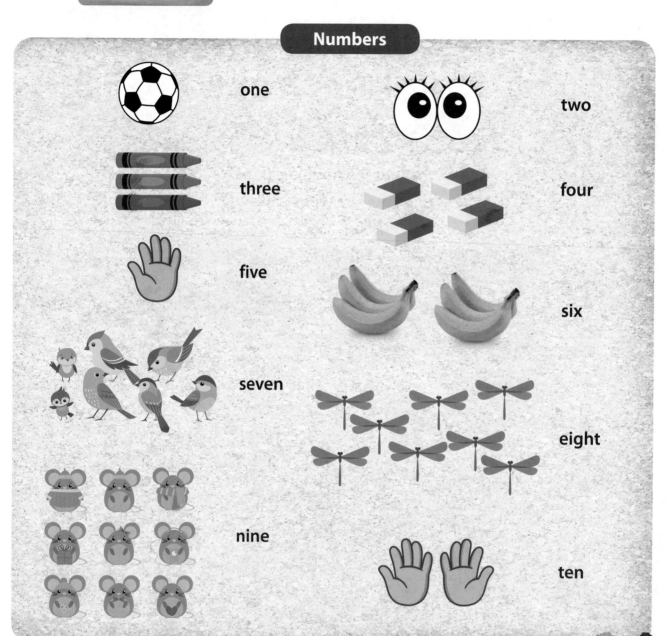

Numbers

one

two

three

four

five

six

seven

eight

nine

ten

ten

one   two   three   four   five   six   seven   eight   nine

Power Verbs

count
Let's **count** the candles.

say aloud
Let's **say** the numbers **aloud**.

Word Families

come before
3 comes before 4.

come after
4 comes after 3.

less than
One is **less than** two. (1 < 2)

more than
Two is **more than** one. (2 > 1)

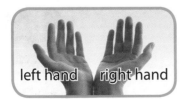

left hand   right hand

hand
You have **two hands**.

finger
You have **ten fingers**.

Now I'm ten years old!

Numbers from 1 to 10

Look at the birthday cake.
How many candles are on it?
One, two, three, four, five.
Six, seven, eight, nine, ten.
There are ten candles. Jack is ten years old.

We use numbers when we count.

 There is **1** dog. There are **3** kittens.

Here are the numbers from 1 to 10.
Let's say each number aloud in order.

1 comes before **2**. **2** comes before **3**.
2 comes after **1**. **3** comes after **2**.

1 2 3 4
▲ The numbers are in order.

3 1 2 4
▲ The numbers are **not** in order.

Now, answer the questions.

How many noses do you have?
One! You have one nose.
How many eyes do you have?
Two! You have two eyes.

One is less than two. Two is more than one.

I have one nose and two eyes.

How many fingers do you have on your left hand?
Five! You have five fingers on your left hand.

How many fingers do you have on your right hand?
Five! You have five fingers on your right hand.

How many fingers do you have on both hands?
Ten! You have ten fingers on both hands.

Five is less than ten. Ten is more than five.

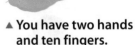
▲ You have two hands and ten fingers.

Check Understanding

1 **Which number does each picture show?**

a

b

_____   _____

2 **How many eyes do you have?**
   a one   b two   c three

3 **Which number comes before 7?**
   a 7   b 5   c 6

4 **8 is _____ 9.**
   a less than   b more than   c comes before

- Answer the questions below.
1 What are the numbers from 1 to 5?
   ⇨ They are _____, _____, _____, _____, and _____.

2 What are the numbers from 6 to 10?
   ⇨ They are _____, _____, _____, _____, and _____.

A **Look, Read, and Write.**
Look at the pictures. Write the correct words.

| before | seven | how many | more than |

1
_____ ears do you have?

2
←
1 2 3 4 5 6
▸ 5 comes _____ 6.

3
▸ There are _____ cats.

4
▸ 8 is _____ 5.

B **More or Less?**
Draw a circle around the right words and then write the words.

1234567 8 9 10

1   One is _____ than two.
        more   less

2   Eight is _____ than four.
        more   less

3   Seven comes _____ three.
        before   after

4   Nine comes _____ ten.
        before   after

78

Unit 11

Lines and Shapes

Reading Focus

- What are some lines?
- What are some shapes?
- How can you make shapes?

Key Words

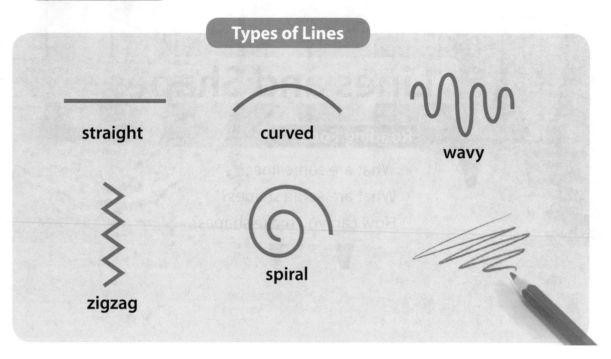

Types of Lines

straight

curved

wavy

zigzag

spiral

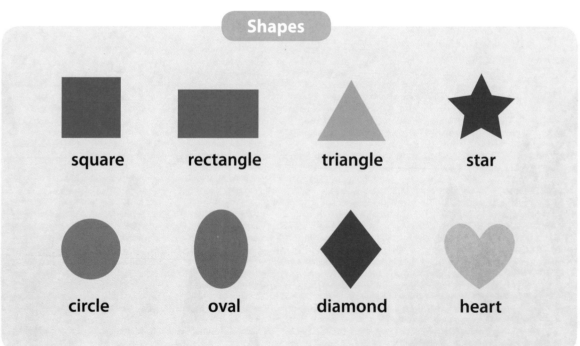

Shapes

square

rectangle

triangle

star

circle

oval

diamond

heart

Power Verbs

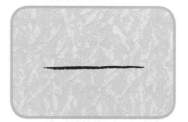

draw
Draw a line.

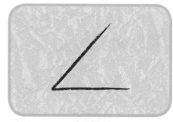

join
You can **join** two lines together.

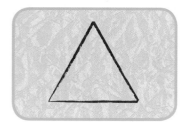

be made of
Shapes **are made of** lines.

name
Can you **name** these shapes?

Word Families

thick   **thin**
round

look alike
They **look alike**.

look different
They **look different**.

pencil   colored pencil   crayon   marker

drawing materials

Lines and Shapes

▲ Mary's drawing

Mary is drawing a house.
Can you see the lines like these: — | ⌇ ?

We use lines when we draw pictures.
Let's say you want to draw a banana.
You might start with a curved line like this.

There are many types of lines.

curved line **straight line** **wavy line** **zigzag line** **spiral line**

Lines can be thin or thick, too.
Use a sharp pencil, and you can make a thin line.
Use a crayon, and you can make a thick line.

▲ thin line

When lines join together, they make shapes.

▲ thick line

Can you name these shapes?
They are a circle, a triangle, a square, and a rectangle.

A circle is round. It is made of a curved line.
A triangle, a square, and a rectangle are made of straight lines.

A square and a rectangle look alike.
A circle and a triangle look different.

Here are four other shapes:
a diamond, a star, a heart, and an oval.

What kinds of lines can you see in the pictures?

spiral line

curved line

zigzag line

Check Understanding

1 **What kinds of lines can you see in the pictures?**

a

b

_____   _____

2 **What kind of line can a pencil make?**
  a a thin line   **b** a thick line   **c** a small line

3 **A _____ and a rectangle look alike?**
  a a circle   **b** a square   **c** a triangle

4 **When lines join together, they make _____.**
  a circles   **b** shapes   **c** hearts

- **Answer the questions below.**

1 What are some different types of lines?
  ⇨ There are _____, _____, _____, _____, and _____ lines.

2 How do a circle and a rectangle look?
  ⇨ A circle and a rectangle look _____.

A **Look, Read, and Write.**
Look at the pictures. Write the correct words.

thick line	made of	drawing	round

1 ▶ He is _____ a picture.

2 ▶ A crayon makes a _____.

3 ▶ A circle is _____.

4 ▶ A square is _____ four straight lines.

B **Alike or Different?**
Draw a circle around the right words and then write the words.

1   A square and a rectangle look _____.
                            alike   different

2   A triangle and a circle look _____.
                       alike   different

3   A zigzag line and a straight line look _____.
                              alike   different

4   A circle and an oval look _____.
                       alike   different

Unit 12

Let's Beat the Drum

Reading Focus

- What are some musical instruments?
- Can you play any musical instruments?
- How do you play those musical instruments?

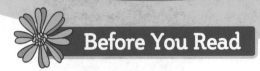
Before You Read

23

Key Words

Musical Instruments

piano

violin

drumstick

stick

drum

triangle

tambourine

stick

xylophone

cymbals

castanets

Power Verbs

play

She can **play** the piano.

hit

Hit the triangle with a stick.

beat

You **beat** the drum.

tap

You **tap** the xylophone.

shake

You **shake** the tambourine.

bang

You **bang** the cymbals.

click

You **click** the castanets.

Let's Beat the Drum

Do you like music?
Do you like to sing and dance?
How about playing an instrument?

There are many musical instruments.
Let's learn about some fun instruments.
What are the names of these instruments?

That's right. They are the drum, triangle, and xylophone.
We call them percussion instruments.

Percussion instruments are fun to play.
You hit them with your hands or a stick.

Can you name another percussion instrument?
Did you think of the tambourine?
The cymbals? The castanets?
That's right. They are all in the percussion family.

▲ percussion family

Let's play them.
The drum has a drumstick.
You beat the drum with the stick.
The xylophone has a stick, too.
You tap the xylophone with the stick.

I'm a drum.
Beat me with a stick.

I'm a xylophone.
Tap me with a stick.

You shake the tambourine with your hands.
You bang the cymbals with your hands.
And you click the castanets with your fingers.

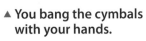
▲ You bang the cymbals with your hands.

▲ You shake the tambourine with your hands.

Check Understanding

1 **Which type of instrument does each picture show?**

a

b

c

d

2 **What do you use to play the drum?**
a a tambourine   b a drumstick   c a triangle

3 **What kind of instrument is the xylophone?**
a a percussion instrument   b a keyboard instrument
c a fun instrument

4 **You _____ the castanets with your fingers.**
a bang   b shake   c click

• **Answer the questions below.**

1 How do you play the cymbals?
⇨ You _____ the cymbals with your hands.

2 How do you play the tambourine?
⇨ You _____ the tambourine with your hands.

A **Look, Read, and Write.**
Look at the pictures. Write the correct words.

drum   percussion   stick   hits

1  ▶ The boy beats the _____.

2  ▶ She _____ the triangle.

3 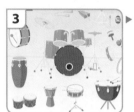 ▶ _____ instruments are fun to play.

4 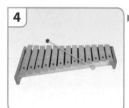 ▶ The xylophone has a _____.

B **Hit or Tap?**
Draw a circle around the right words and then write the words.

1 You _____ the piano with your fingers.
shake   play

2 You _____ the xylophone with a stick.
click   tap

3 You _____ the cymbals.
bang   shake

4 You _____ the tambourine.
click   shake

A Look at the pictures. Write the correct words.

| after | made of | harvested | drumstick |

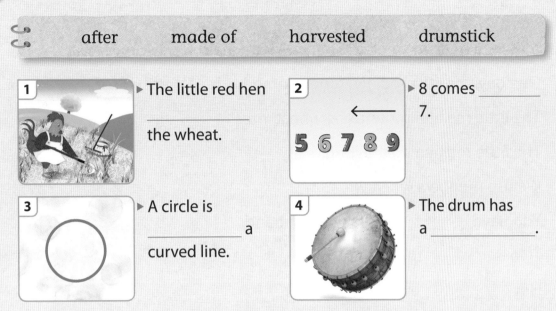

1 ▶ The little red hen _____ the wheat.

2 ▶ 8 comes _____ 7.

5 6 7 8 9

3 ▶ A circle is _____ a curved line.

4 ▶ The drum has a _____.

B Draw a circle around the right words and then write the words.

6 > 4

1 The little red hen _____ the wheat into flour.

ground   grounded

2 Six is _____ than four.

more   less

3 A square and a rectangle look _____.

alike   different

4 You _____ the castanets with your fingers.

shake   click

91

C Complete the sentences with the words below.

farm	flour	many	ten
less	count	by herself	grains

1 A little red hen lived on a _____ with a pig, a duck, and a cat.

2 One day, the little red hen found some _____ of wheat.

3 The little red hen ground the wheat into _____.

4 The little red hen ate the bread all _____.

5 We use numbers when we _____.

6 You have _____ fingers on both hands.

7 Two is _____ than three.

8 How _____ eyes do you have?

D Complete the sentences with the words below.

shapes	tap	alike	stick
draw	different	percussion	shake

1 We use lines when we _____ pictures.

2 When lines join together, they make _____.

3 A circle and an oval look _____.

4 A circle and a triangle look _____.

5 Drums and triangles are _____ instruments.

6 You hit percussion instruments with your hands or a _____.

7 You _____ the xylophone with a stick .

8 You _____ the tambourine with your hands.

92

Word
List

Word List

01 Seasons and Weather
季節與天氣

1	look	看
2	outside	外面
3	sunny	晴朗的
4	cloudy	多雲的
5	weather	天氣
6	change	變化
7	from day to day	一日復一日；每天
8	can be	可以是……
9	rainy	下雨的
10	snowy	下雪的
11	season	季節
12	from season to season	隨著季節更替
13	year	年
14	four seasons	四季
15	spring	春天
16	summer	夏天
17	fall	秋天 (= autumn)
18	winter	冬天
19	warm	溫暖的
20	flower	花 * 複數：flowers
21	begin to	開始……
22	bloom	盛開
23	come after	在……之後來臨
24	hot	熱的
25	the warmest	最溫暖的 *warm–warmer–warmest
26	cooler	較涼爽的 *cool–cooler–coolest
27	than	（比較級用法）比……
28	leaf	葉子
29	leaves	葉子（複數）
30	change colors	變化顏色
31	cold	冷的
32	the coldest	最冷的 *cold–colder–coldest

02 Our Land and Water
我們的土地與水

1	Earth	地球
2	be made up of	由……所組成
3	land	土地；陸地
4	water	水
5	picture	圖片
6	tell	分辨
7	which part	哪個部分
8	kind	種類
9	different kinds of	有不同種類的……
10	mountain	山
11	the highest	最高的 *high–higher–highest
12	form	形狀；外形
13	form of land	地形
14	hill	丘陵
15	lower than	比……來得低 *low–lower–lowest
16	valley	山谷
17	low	低的
18	between	在……之間
19	usually	通常
20	narrow	狹窄的
21	flat	平坦的
22	be called	被稱為……
23	plain	平原
24	be good for	適合於……
25	farming	農耕
26	desert	沙漠
27	dry	乾燥的
28	very little rain	很少下雨
29	island	島嶼
30	be surrounded by	被……圍繞
31	ocean	海洋
32	the largest	最大的 *large–larger–largest
33	body of water	水域
34	cover	覆蓋
35	much of	很多的
36	lake	湖泊
37	large	大的
38	river	河流
39	long	長的
40	flow into	流進……裡

03 Many Jobs
多種多樣的職業

1	my home	我家
2	lots of	很多
3	job	職業；工作
4	help	幫助
5	feed	餵食
6	water	澆（水）
7	plant	植物
8	my mom	我媽媽
9	cook	煮
10	dinner	晚餐
11	work	工作
12	earn	賺（錢）
13	there are	有……

14	many kinds of	很多種……
15	farmer	農夫
16	grow	種植
17	fruit	水果
18	vegetable	蔬菜
19	worker	工人
20	factory	工廠 * 複數：factories
21	service job	服務業
22	waiter	服務生 *waitress 女服務生
23	serve	服務；侍候
24	restaurant	餐廳
25	doctor	醫生
26	be sick	生病
27	work for	為……工作
28	community	社會大眾
29	firefighter	消防人員
30	put out	撲滅（火）
31	dangerous	危險的
32	fire	火
33	police officer	警察
34	safety	安全
35	volunteer	義工
36	for free	免費
37	homeless	無家可歸的
38	hospital	醫院
39	all kinds of	所有種類的……
40	important	重要的
41	what kind of	什麼種類
42	would like to	想要……

04 Transportation
交通工具

1	student	學生
2	ride	騎（機車、腳踏車等）
3	bike	腳踏車 (= bicycle)
4	school	學校
5	sometimes	有時候
6	take	搭乘（公車、校車等）
7	school bus	校車
8	transportation	交通工具
9	move	移動
10	thing	物品
11	from one place to another	從某地到其他地方去
12	drive	開（車、公車等）
13	work	工作
14	subway	地下鐵
15	a lot of	很多
16	at one time	一次、同時間
17	delivery truck	貨運卡車
18	deliver	運送
19	tanker truck	油罐車
20	carry	載運
21	oil	石油
22	gas	汽油
23	train	火車
24	airplane	飛機
25	helicopter	直升機
26	in the air	在空中
27	fly	飛

28	around the world	全世界
29	transport	運送
30	goods	貨品
31	travel	旅遊
32	on the water	在水面上
33	ship	船
34	ferry	渡輪

05 A World of Plants
植物世界

1	garden	花園
2	grow	種植
3	plant	植物
4	different	不同的
5	many different kinds of	很多種不同的……
6	big	大的
7	small	小的
8	grass	青草
9	vegetable	蔬菜 * 複數：vegetables
10	tree	樹 * 複數：trees
11	part	部分
12	root	根
13	stem	莖
14	leaf	葉 * 複數：leaves
15	flower	花 * 複數：flowers
16	fruit	水果；果實
17	hold	包含

18	seed	種子
19	radish	甜菜根 * 複數：radishes
20	onion	洋蔥
21	carrot	胡蘿蔔
22	celery	芹菜
23	such as	像是……（舉例說明）
24	lettuce	萵苣
25	cabbage	甘藍菜
26	broccoli	綠花椰菜
27	cauliflower	白花椰菜
28	apple	蘋果
29	pear	梨子
30	strawberry	草莓 * 複數：strawberries
31	sometimes	有時候
32	corn	玉米
33	rice	稻穀
34	peanut	花生

06 A World of Animals
動物世界

1	favorite	最喜歡的
2	animal	動物
3	like	喜歡
4	dog	狗
5	cat	貓
6	tiny	非常小的
7	like	像是……
8	ant	螞蟻

9	huge	巨大的
10	elephant	大象
11	need	需要
12	food	食物
13	live	生存；生活
14	air	空氣
15	lung	肺

* 複數：lungs（多用複數，因為肺通常有兩顆）

16	help	幫助
17	breathe	呼吸
18	gill	（魚）鰓

* 複數：gills（多用複數，因為魚鰓通常有兩個）

19	fish	魚
20	place	地方
21	forest	森林
22	bear	熊
23	squirrel	松鼠
24	deer	鹿
25	grassland	草原
26	giraffe	長頸鹿
27	lion	獅子
28	snake	蛇
29	lizard	蜥蜴
30	desert	沙漠
31	a few	一些（為數不多）
32	polar bear	北極熊
33	the North Pole	北極
34	penguin	企鵝
35	the South Pole	南極

36	shark	鯊魚
37	whale	鯨魚
38	dolphin	海豚

07 A World of Insects
昆蟲世界

1	look at	看……
2	picture	圖片
3	name	說出（名字）
4	each of	各個的……
5	ant	螞蟻
6	honeybee	蜜蜂
7	butterfly	蝴蝶
8	beetle	甲蟲
9	insect	昆蟲
10	come in	有……（接狀態）
11	color	顏色
12	shape	形狀
13	size	尺寸
14	body part	身體部位
15	head	頭部
16	thorax	胸部
17	abdomen	腹部
18	leg	腳
19	wing	翅膀
20	fly	飛
21	bee	蜜蜂
22	both	（兩者）都
23	take a look at	看一看

24 close	關閉		17 smell	嗅覺
25 divide	分類		18 taste	味覺
26 be divided into	將……分為		19 touch	觸覺
27 antenna	觸角 * 複數：antennae		20 see	看
			21 know	知道
28 touch	觸碰		22 look	看
29 smell	聞		23 hear	聽
30 only	只有		24 take in	接收
31 queen ant	蟻后		25 sound	聲音
32 male ant	雄蟻		26 understand	了解
			27 tell	告訴
			28 tongue	舌頭

08 What Are the Five Senses?
何謂五種官能？

1 hear	聽		29 if	如果
2 alarm clock	鬧鐘		30 sweet	甜的
3 ring	（鬧鐘、鈴聲）響 *ringing 聲響		31 sour	酸的
			32 salty	鹹的
4 in the morning	早上的時候		33 bitter	苦的
5 wake up	醒來		34 chocolate	巧克力
6 look around	看看周圍		35 lemon	檸檬
7 smell	聞		36 finger	手指
8 breakfast	早餐		37 skin	皮膚
9 get up	起床		38 feel	感覺
10 taste	嚐		39 smooth	光滑的
11 use	使用		40 rough	粗糙的
12 sense	官能		41 teddy bear	泰迪熊
13 every day	每天		42 stove	火爐
14 five senses	五種官能			
15 sight	視覺			
16 hearing	聽覺			

09 The Little Red Hen
紅色小母雞

1	once upon a time	很久很久以前
2	hen	母雞
3	farm	農場
4	live with	跟……住在一起
5	pig	豬
6	duck	鴨子
7	cat	貓咪
8	work hard	勤奮工作
9	never	從不;從來沒有
10	one day	有一天
11	find	發現 * 過去式:found
12	grain	穀粒
13	wheat	小麥
14	plant	種植
15	think	想 * 過去式:thought
16	ask	詢問 * 過去式:asked
17	oink	齁齁(豬叫聲) * 過去式:oinked
18	quack	呱呱(鴨子叫聲) * 過去式:quacked
19	meow	喵喵(貓叫聲) * 過去式:meowed
20	very well (then)	那好吧
21	myself	我自己
22	cluck	咕咕 * 過去式:clucked
23	grow	長大;生長 * 過去式:grew

24	turn	變成
25	golden color	金黃色
26	be ready to	準備好
27	harvest	收成
28	be harvested	被收割
29	cut	割 * 過去式:cut
30	grind...into...	磨碎……變成……
31	flour	麵粉
32	ground	磨碎 *grind 的過去式
33	bake	烘焙;烤
34	bread	麵包
35	finally	最後
36	come out of	從……出來 * 過去式:came out of
37	oven	烤爐
38	look	看起來
39	delicious	可口
40	won't	將不會 *will not 的縮寫
41	all by myself	全部都靠我自己
42	all by herself	全部都靠她自己

10 Numbers from 1 to 10
數字 1 到 10

1	look at	看……
2	birthday cake	生日蛋糕
3	candle	蠟燭
4	ten years old	十歲
5	use	使用

6	number	數字	
7	count	計算	
8	There is/are	有……	
9	kitten	小貓	
10	from 1 to 10	從 1 到 10	
11	say aloud	大聲說出來	
12	in order	照順序	
13	come before	在……之前來臨	
14	come after	在……之後來臨	
15	answer	回答	
16	question	問題	
17	nose	鼻子	
18	eye	眼睛	
19	less than	比……少	
20	more than	比……多	
21	finger	手指	
22	left hand	左手	
23	right hand	右手	
24	both hands	兩隻手	

11 Lines and Shapes
線條與形狀

1	draw	畫（圖）
2	line	線條
3	draw pictures	畫畫
4	let's say	如果說；比如
5	might	也許
6	start with	用……開始
7	curved line	弧線

8	type	種類
9	types of lines	線條的種類
10	straight line	直線
11	wavy line	波浪狀線條
12	zigzag line	鋸齒狀線條
13	spiral line	螺旋狀線條
14	thin	細的
15	thick	粗的
16	sharp	尖的
17	pencil	鉛筆
18	thin line	細線條
19	crayon	蠟筆
20	thick line	粗線條
21	join together	集合在一起
22	shape	形狀
23	name	叫出（名字）
24	circle	圓形
25	triangle	三角形
26	square	正方形
27	rectangle	長方形
28	round	圓的
29	be made of	由……組成
30	look alike	看起來相似
31	look different	看起來不同
32	diamond	菱形
33	star	星；星形
34	heart	心；心形
35	oval	橢圓形

12 Let's Beat the Drum
大家一起來打鼓

1 **music** 音樂

2 **like to** 喜歡（去做某事）

3 **sing** 唱歌

4 **dance** 跳舞

5 **How about V-ing?** 那覺得……怎麼樣？

6 **play** 演奏

7 **instrument** 樂器

8 **musical instrument** 樂器

9 **learn about** 認識……

10 **fun** 有趣的

11 **That's right.** 沒錯！

12 **drum** 鼓

13 **triangle** 三角鐵

14 **xylophone** 木琴

15 **call** 稱為

16 **percussion instrument** 打擊樂器

17 **hit** 敲打

18 **stick** 棒子；鼓棒；琴棒

19 **think of** 認為

20 **tambourine** 鈴鼓

21 **cymbals** 鐃鈸

22 **castanets** 響板

23 **percussion family** 打擊樂器家族

24 **easy** 簡單的

25 **drumstick** 鼓棒

26 **beat** 敲打

27 **tap** 輕輕敲擊

28 **shake** 搖晃

29 **bang** 撞擊

30 **click** 輕點（按）

Unit 01 Seasons and Weather

季節與天氣

Reading Focus 閱讀焦點

- What are the four seasons? 四季是哪四季？
- What are some kinds of weather? 天氣有哪些種類？
- How does weather change? 天氣是如何變化的？

Key Words 關鍵字彙

sunny 晴朗的

Weather 天氣

cloudy 多雲的

rainy 下雨的

snowy 下雪的

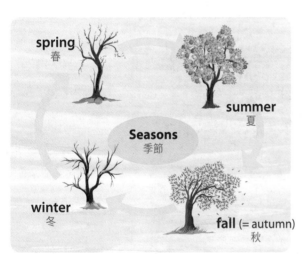

spring 春

summer 夏

Seasons 季節

winter 冬

fall (= autumn) 秋

Power Verbs 核心動詞

rain 下雨

It is **raining**.
現在正在下雨。

snow 下雪

It is **snowing**.
現在正在下雪。

bloom 盛開

Flowers **bloom**.
百花盛開。

change 改變

Leaves **change** colors.
葉子換了顏色。

Word Families: Comparative and Superlative

相關字彙：比較級和最高級

hot	<	hotter	<	hottest
熱的		比較熱的		最熱的

cold	<	colder	<	coldest
冷的		比較冷的		最冷的

warm	<	warmer	<	warmest
溫暖的		比較溫暖的		最溫暖的

cool	<	cooler	<	coolest
涼爽的		比較涼爽的		最涼爽的

Seasons and Weather 季節與天氣

看看外頭，
是晴天？還是陰天？

天氣一天一天在改變，
它可以是晴天，
它可以是陰天，
它可以是雨天或下雪天。

天氣也隨著季節更替而改變。
一年有四個季節，
分別是春天、夏天、秋天和冬天。

春天很溫暖，
百花在春天綻放。

夏天緊跟春天之後到來，
夏天非常炎熱而且艷陽高照，
這是最溫暖的季節。

秋天隨著夏天之後來臨，
秋天比夏天來得涼爽，
葉子在秋天換上新色彩。

冬天跟隨秋天之後來到，
冬天非常寒冷而且雪花紛飛，
這是最冷冽的季節。

Check Understanding 文意測驗

1 下列圖片中分別是哪一個季節？
  a spring 春   b winter 冬

2 那個季節最寒冷？ c
  a 夏天   b 秋天   c 冬天

3 在秋天，樹會發生什麼變化？ b
  a 百花綻放   b 葉子換上新色彩   c 樹葉轉綠

4 夏天是_____的季節。 a
  a 炎熱   b 涼爽   c 雪花紛飛

● 回答問題。

1 What are the four seasons? 四季是哪四季？
  ⇨ They are spring, summer, fall, and winter. 分別是春、夏、秋和冬。

2 Which season comes after winter? 哪一個季節會在冬天之後來到？
  ⇨ Spring comes after winter. 春天在冬天之後來到。

Vocabulary and Grammar Builder 字彙與文法練習

Ⓐ 看圖填空：依照圖片選出正確的單字。

  1 The weather can be cloudy. 天氣可能是陰天。

  2 The weather can be rainy. 天氣可能是雨天。

  3 Flowers bloom in spring. 百花在春天綻放。

  4 Leaves change colors in fall. 葉子在秋天換上新色彩。

Ⓑ 比較級和最高級：請圈出正確的單字，並將答案填在空格中。

  1 Spring is ____warmer____ than winter. 春天比冬天來得溫暖。
     cooler ⟨warmer⟩

  2 Summer is the ____warmest____ season. 夏天是最溫暖的季節。
     coolest ⟨warmest⟩

  3 Fall is ____cooler____ than summer. 秋天比夏天來得涼爽。
     ⟨cooler⟩ warmer

  4 Winter is the ____coldest____ season. 冬天是最冷冽的季節。
     ⟨coldest⟩ warmest

Unit 02 Our Land and Water

我們的土地與水

Reading Focus 閱讀焦點

- What are some kinds of land? 土地有哪些形式？
- What are some kinds of water? 水有哪些形式？
- How are they different? 這些地形有何不同？

Key Words 關鍵字彙

mountain
山

hill
丘陵

valley
山谷

Kinds of Land
地形

plain
平原

desert
沙漠

island
島嶼

Kinds of Water 水域

ocean
海洋

lake
湖泊

river
河流

Power Verbs 核心動詞

be made up of
由……所組成

Earth **is made up of** land and water.
地球是由陸地和水所組成。

be surrounded by
被……環繞

An island **is surrounded by** water.
島嶼四周被水環繞。

*surround 環繞

cover
覆蓋

Oceans **cover** much of our Earth.
海洋覆蓋了大半個地球。

flow into
流進……

Rivers **flow into** oceans.
河流滾滾流進海洋。

Word Families: The Adjectives for Land
相關字彙；地形的形容詞

mountain
山

hill
丘陵

high < higher
高的   比較高的

low < lower
低的   比較低的

plain
平原

valley
山谷

desert
沙漠

flat
平坦的

narrow
狹窄的

dry
乾燥的

106

Our Land and Water 我們的土地與水

地球是由陸地和水所組成。
這是一張地球的圖片,
你能不能分辨哪些部分是陸地?
哪些部分是水?

地球上的土地有很多不同的形式:
山峰是最高的地形,
丘陵比山峰來得低一點。
山谷是高山之間的低地,
而且山谷通常是狹窄的地形。

有些土地平坦,
我們稱這種土地為平原,
平原的地形適合農耕。

沙漠是一片乾燥的土地,
沙漠中很少有雨水滋潤。
不過島嶼卻是四周被水環繞。

地球上的水有很多不同的形式:
海洋是地球上佔地最大、最廣的水域,
覆蓋了大半個地球。

湖泊是一片面積寬闊的水域,
四周被土地環繞。

河流是一道長長的水域,
滾滾流進海洋。

Check Understanding 文意測驗

1 下列圖片中分別是哪一種地形?
   a **desert** 沙漠   b **island** 島嶼

2 哪一個是最低的地形? **b**
   a 丘陵   b 平原   c 山峰

3 高山之間的低地被稱為什麼? **a**
   a 山谷   b 平原   c 丘陵

4 _____四周被陸地圍繞。 **a**
   a 湖泊   b 河流   c 島嶼

● 回答問題。

1 What are some different kinds of land? 土地有哪些形式?
   ⇨ **Mountains**, hills, **valleys**, **plains**, deserts, and **islands** are kinds of land.
   有山峰、丘陵、山谷、平原、沙漠和島嶼這些地形。

2 What are some different kinds of water? 水有哪些形式?
   ⇨ **Oceans**, **lakes**, and **rivers** are kinds of water. 有海洋、湖泊、河流這些形式。

Vocabulary and Grammar Builder 字彙與文法練習

Ⓐ 看圖填空:依照圖片選出正確的單字。

1 A hill is **lower** than a mountain. 丘陵比山峰來得低。

2 A valley is usually **narrow**. 山谷通常是狹窄的地形。

3 A desert is a **dry** land. 沙漠是乾燥的土地。

4 A plain is good for **farming**. 平原適合農耕。

Ⓑ 介系詞:圈出正確的單字,並填入空格中。

1 Earth is made up ___of___ land and water. 地球是由陸地和水所組成。
   (of) on

2 An island is surrounded ___by___ water. 島嶼四周被水圍繞。
   at (by)

3 A river flows ___into___ an ocean. 河流滾滾流進海洋。
   (into) onto

4 A valley is ___between___ two mountains. 山谷在兩座山峰之間。
   under (between)

107

Unit 03 Many Jobs

多種多樣的職業

Reading Focus 閱讀焦點

- What is a job? 職業是什麼？
- Why do people work? 為什麼人們要工作？
- What are some jobs that people do? 人們都從事哪些職業？
- What are some jobs that volunteers do? 義工都從事哪些工作？

Key Words 關鍵字彙

waiter
服務生

Service Jobs
服務業

doctor
醫生

bus driver
公車司機

deliveryman
快遞人員

Community Jobs
服務大眾的工作

police officer
警察

firefighter
消防員

mail carrier
郵差

Volunteers
義工

help others
幫助他人

work for free
免費服務

Power Verbs 核心動詞

work
工作

He **works** hard.
他工作很努力。

earn
賺（錢）

People **earn** money at work.
人們為了賺錢而工作。

feed
餵（食）

I **feed** my dog.
我會餵我的狗兒。

water
澆（水）

I **water** plants.
我會澆花。

serve
服務

A waiter **serves** food.
服務生端菜。

Word Families: What They Do?
相關字彙：他們都做些什麼？

Jobs 職業	What They Do 他們都做些什麼？
farmers 農夫	grow fruits and vegetables 種植水果和蔬菜
doctors 醫生	help sick people 幫助生病的人們
waiters 服務生	serve food at restaurants 在餐廳為客人端菜
firefighters 消防員	put out fires 撲滅惡火

108

Many Jobs 多種多樣的職業

我叫做約翰，這裡是我家。
我在家裡幫忙做很多工作，
我會餵我的狗兒、澆花，
還會幫媽媽煮晚餐。

在家裡，你都做些什麼工作？

職業是人們從事的工作，
大部分的人們工作都是為了賺錢。

職業的種類繁多，
農夫種植蔬菜、水果，
有些人則是在工廠裡工作。

有些人從事服務業，
服務生在餐廳裡為客人上菜，
醫生幫助生病的人們。

有些人為社會大眾工作，
消防員撲滅危險的惡火，
警察為了大眾的安全而努力。

有些工作者志願當義工，
義工的工作是免費服務需要幫助的人。
有些義工會分送食物給無家可歸的人們，
有些義工在醫院裡奉獻心力。

所有的工作都佔有一席之地。
你最想從事哪一種工作呢？

Check Understanding 文意測驗

1 下列圖片中分別是哪些職業？
　a **doctor** 醫生　　　b **firefighter** 消防員

2 大部分的人工作是為了什麼？ **b**
　a 為了替客人上菜　　　b 為了賺錢　　　c 為了幫助病人

3 義工的工作是什麼？ **c**
　a 在工廠裡工作　　　b 賺錢　　　c 幫助別人

4 _____為了大眾的安全而工作。 **c**
　a 農夫　　　b 服務生　　　c 警察

● 回答問題。

1 What are some jobs that people do at home? 在家裡，人們會做哪些工作？
　⇨ Some people <u>feed</u> their dogs and <u>water</u> their plants. 有些人餵他們的狗兒和澆花。

2 What are some jobs that volunteers do? 義工做些什麼工作？
　⇨ They <u>serve</u> food to homeless people or work at <u>hospitals</u>.
　　他們分送食物給無家可歸的人，或是在醫院奉獻心力。

Vocabulary and Grammar Builder 字彙與文法練習

🅐 看圖填空：依照圖片選出正確的單字。

　1 Most people have jobs to <u>earn money</u>. 大部分的人為了賺錢而工作。

　2 <u>Police officers</u> work for the community. 警察為社會大眾工作。

　3 Volunteers <u>work for free</u> to help others. 義工免費幫助別人。

　4 Some workers work in <u>factories</u>. 有些人在工廠裡工作。

🅑 他們從事什麼工作？圈出正確的單字，並填入空格中。

　1 Farmers ___**grow**___ fruits and vegetables. 農夫種植水果和蔬菜。
　　(grow)　cook

　2 Waiters ___**serve food**___ at restaurants. 服務生在餐廳裡端菜。
　　(serve food)　work for free

　3 Doctors ___**help**___ people who are sick. 醫生幫助生病的人們。
　　feed　(help)

　4 Firefighters ___**put out**___ dangerous fires. 消防員撲滅危險的惡火。
　　(put out)　put on

Unit 04 Transportation
交通工具

Reading Focus 閱讀焦點

• What is transportation? 何謂交通工具？

• Why do people use transportation? 為什麼人們要使用交通工具？

• What kinds of transportation are there? 交通工具有哪些？

Key Words 關鍵字彙

car
汽車

bicycle(=bike)
腳踏車

bus
公車

Land Transportation
陸上交通工具

train
火車

subway
地下鐵

truck
卡車

Air Transportation
空中交通工具

airplane
飛機

helicopter
直升機

jet
噴射機

Water Transportation
水上交通工具

ship
船

ferry
渡輪

cargo ship
貨船

Power Verbs 核心動詞

ride
騎（腳踏車、機車等）

She **rides** her bike.
她騎自己的腳踏車。

take
搭乘（巴士、校車等）

They **take** the school bus.
他們搭校車。

carry
載運

Trains **carry** many things
at one time.
火車可以一次載運很多東西。

transport
搭載

Ferries **transport** people.
渡輪搭載人們。

Word Families 相關字彙

a bus driver
公車司機
➡ drives a bus
駕駛公車

a delivery truck
貨運卡車
➡ delivers things
遞送貨品

an airplane
飛機
➡ flies in the air
在空中翱翔

a ship
船
➡ moves on the water
在水面上移動

Transportation 交通工具

珍妮是個學生，
她騎腳踏車上學，
不過有時候也會搭校車。

腳踏車和校車就是她的交通工具。
交通工具將人們或物品從某個地方運送到其他地方。

你都使用哪些交通工具？

有些人自己開車上班，
有些人搭地鐵去上班，
有些人搭公車去上班。

有些交通工具可以一次載運大量的物品。
貨運卡車為人們遞送物品，
油罐車運送石油和汽油，
火車也可以一次載運很多東西。

飛機和直升機在空中翱翔，
飛機可以運送人們或貨物到世界各地。

我們也可以在水面上漫遊，
很多船隻和渡輪都會載運人和物品。

Check Understanding 文意測驗

1 下圖中分別是哪一種交通工具？
   a **car** 汽車　　　　　　**b** **airplane** 飛機

2 什麼將人們或物品從某個地方運送到其他地方？ **b**
   a 食物　　　　　　**b** 交通工具　　　　　　**c** 購物中心

3 油罐車都載運些什麼？ **a**
   a 石油和汽油　　　　　　**b** 人們　　　　　　**c** 郵件

4 ＿＿＿＿＿＿在空中翱翔。 **b**
   a 渡輪　　　　　　**b** 直升機　　　　　　**c** 貨運卡車

● 回答問題。

1 Why do people use transportation? 為什麼人們要使用交通工具？
   ⇨ People use transportation to **move** from one place to **another**.
   人們從某個地方搭乘交通工具到其他地方去。

2 What kinds of transportation move on the water? 哪些交通工具在水上移動？
   ⇨ **Ships** and **ferries** move on the water. 船和渡輪在水上移動。

Vocabulary and Grammar Builder 字彙與文法練習

Ⓐ 看圖填空：依照圖片選出正確的單字。

1 A car is one type of **transportation**. 汽車是交通工具的一種。

2 Trucks **carry/transport** many things at one time. 卡車可以一次載運大量的物品。

3 Some people take **buses** to work. 有些人搭公車去上班。

4 Ferries **carry/transport** people or goods. 渡輪載送人們或物品。

Ⓑ 單複數動詞：圈出正確的單字，並填入空格中。

1 Jenny ___**rides**___ her bike to school. 珍妮騎腳踏車去學校。
   ride (rides)

2 Some people ___**take**___ the subway to work. 有些人搭地鐵去上班。
   (take) takes

3 A helicopter ___**flies**___ in the sky. 直升機在空中飛行。
   fly (flies)

4 A delivery truck ___**delivers**___ things to people. 貨運卡車為人們遞送物品。
   deliver (delivers)

Unit 05

A World of Plants
植物世界

Reading Focus 閱讀焦點

- What are some kinds of plants? 植物分成哪些種類？
- What are some parts of a plant? 植物有哪些部位？
- What plant parts do we eat? 植物有哪些部位可供我們食用？

Key Words 關鍵字彙

grass 青草

trees 樹

Kinds of Plants 植物的種類

flowers 花

vegetables 蔬菜

Power Verbs 核心動詞

grow 種植
I **grow** plants.
我種植植物。

live 生存
Plants **live** in many places.
植物可以在很多地方生存。

hold 包含
The fruits **hold** seeds.
果實含有種子。

Word Families:
The Parts of Plants
相關字彙：植物的部位

 roots 根

Some **roots** are **thick**.
有些根很粗。

Some **roots** are **thin**.
有些根很細。

 stems 莖

Some **stems** are **thick**.
有些莖很粗。

Some **stems** are **thin**.
有些莖很細。

 leaves 葉

Some **leaves** are **big**.
有些葉子很大。

Some **leaves** are **little**.
有些葉子很小。

 fruits 果實

Some plants **have** fruits.
有些植物會結果實。

Some plants **do not have** fruits.
有些植物不會結果實。

 seeds 種子

Some **seeds** are **big**.
有些種子很大。

Some **seeds** are **small**.
有些種子很小。

The Parts of a Plant
植物的部位

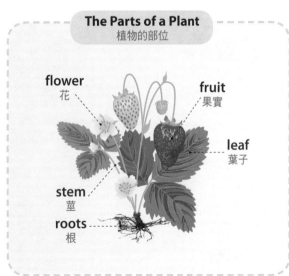

flower 花

fruit 果實

leaf 葉子

stem 莖

roots 根

A World of Plants 植物世界

我叫做史考特,這裡是我的花園,
我在裡面種了很多植物。

植物有許多不同的種類,
植物可以很高大,也可以很小。
青草、蔬菜還有樹木都是植物。

植物分成幾個不同的部位,
大部分的植物都有根、莖、葉三個部分,
也有很多植物會開花,
花會結出果實,
果實裡則含有種子。

植物的很多部位都可供我們食用。

我們可以吃植物的根部,
甜菜根、洋蔥、胡蘿蔔都是植物的根。
我們可以吃植物的莖部,
芹菜就是植物的莖。

我們也會吃葉子,像是萵苣、甘藍菜。
我們也會吃花,像是綠花椰菜、白花椰菜。

大部分的植物果實也可供我們食用,
蘋果、梨子、草莓就是我們會吃的果實。

有時候我們也會吃植物的種子,
玉米、稻穀、花生都是植物的種子。

Check Understanding 文意測驗

1 下列圖片中分別是植物的哪些部位?

   a These are both <u>leaves</u>. 它們都是葉子。　　b These are both <u>stems</u>. 它們都是莖。
   ▊ These are both <u>roots</u>. 它們都是根。

2 花會結出什麼? **c**

   a 莖　　　　　　　　b 葉子　　　　　　　　c 果實

3 下列哪一種植物的花可供我們食用? **b**

   a 玉米　　　　　　　b 綠花椰菜　　　　　　c 胡蘿蔔

4 玉米和稻穀的_____可供我們食用。 **a**

   a 種子　　　　　　　b 莖　　　　　　　　　c 葉子

● 回答問題。

1 What parts do most plants have? 植物分為哪些部位?
   ⇨ Most plants have <u>roots</u>, <u>stems</u>, and <u>leaves</u>. 大部分的植物都有根、莖、葉三個部分。

2 What are some roots that people eat? 哪些植物的根部可以供我們食用?
   ⇨ People eat <u>radishes</u>, <u>onions</u> and <u>carrots</u>. 我們可以吃甜菜根、洋蔥和胡蘿蔔。

Vocabulary and Grammar Builder 字彙與文法練習

Ⓐ 看圖填空:依照圖片選出正確的單字。

1 <u>Vegetables</u> are kinds of plants. 蔬菜是植物的其中一些種類。

2 The fruits <u>hold</u> seeds. 果實裡含有種子。

3 People <u>grow</u> different kinds of plants. 人們種植各種不同的植物。

4 Sometimes we eat the <u>seeds</u> of plants. 有時候我們會吃植物的種子。

Ⓑ 單複數:圈出正確的單字,並填入空格中。

1 a ___**leaf**___ 一片葉子　　　many ___**leaves**___ 很多片葉子
   (leaf) leaves　　　　　　　　　leaf (leaves)

2 A ___**radish**___ is the root of a plant. 甜菜根是植物的根。
   (radish) radishes

3 ___**Corns**___ are delicious seeds. 玉米是好吃的種子。
   A corn (Corns)

4 ___**Strawberries**___ are fruits we eat. 草莓是我們會吃的果實。
   A strawberry (Strawberries)

113

Unit 06
A World of Animals
動物世界

Reading Focus 閱讀焦點

• What are some kinds of animals? 動物有哪些種類？

• Where do these animals live? 這些動物都住在哪裡？

• What do animals need to live? 動物需要什麼才能生存？

Key Words 關鍵字彙

Land Animals
陸生動物

squirrel
松鼠

snake
蛇

polar bear
北極熊

deer
鹿

lizard
蜥蜴

penguin
企鵝

giraffe
長頸鹿

Water Animals
水生動物

goldfish
金魚

shark
鯊魚

whale
鯨魚

dolphin
海豚

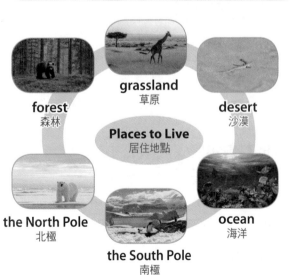

forest
森林

grassland
草原

desert
沙漠

Places to Live
居住地點

the North Pole
北極

the South Pole
南極

ocean
海洋

Power Verbs 核心動詞

need
需要

breathe
呼吸

Animals **need** food and water.
動物需要食物和水。

Land animals **breathe** air.
陸生動物會呼吸空氣。

Word Families 相關字彙

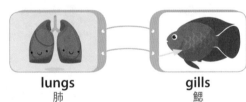

lungs
肺

gills
鰓

Lungs help animals breathe.
肺幫助動物呼吸。

Gills help fish breathe.
鰓幫助魚類呼吸。

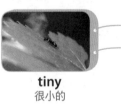

tiny
很小的

huge
巨大的

Ants are **tiny**.
螞蟻很小。

Elephants are **huge**.
大象很巨大。

favorite
最喜歡的

like
喜歡

My **favorite** animals are dogs.
我最喜歡的動物是狗。

I **like** dogs.
我喜歡狗。

A World of Animals 動物世界

你最喜歡的動物是什麼？
你喜歡狗嗎？還是你喜歡貓？

動物有很多不同的種類，
有些動物像螞蟻一樣小，
有些動物又像大象一樣巨大。

動物需要水跟食物才能生存。
有些動物是草食性，
有些動物則獵食其他的動物。

動物也需要空氣，他們使用肺呼吸，
而魚在水中是使用鰓呼吸。

所有的動物也都需要生活空間，

動物們分別住在不一樣的地方。

有很多動物住在森林裡，
熊、松鼠還有鹿都是森林的居民。

有些動物住在草原，
長頸鹿、大象和獅子都住在大草原上。

有些動物則是住在沙漠裡，像是蛇和蜥蜴。

有少數的動物住在非常寒冷的地方。
北極熊住在北極，而企鵝住在南極。

魚則是住在水中，
鯊魚、鯨魚還有海豚都在大海中生活。

Check Understanding 文意測驗

1 下列圖片中分別是什麼地方？
   a **grassland** 草原   **b** **the North Pole** 北極

2 下列哪一個是很大的動物？ **a**
   a 大象   **b** 螞蟻   **c** 狗

3 什麼動物住在森林裡？ **c**
   a 企鵝   **b** 金魚   **c** 鹿

4 動物使用_____呼吸空氣。 **b**
   a 鰓   **b** 肺   **c** 心臟

● 回答問題。

1 Which animals live in grasslands? 哪些動物住在草原上？
   ⇨ <u>Giraffes</u>, <u>elephants</u>, and lions live in grasslands. 長頸鹿、大象和獅子都住在草原上。

2 Where do penguins live? 企鵝住在哪裡？
   ⇨ Penguins live at the <u>South</u> <u>Pole</u>. 企鵝住在南極。

Vocabulary and Grammar Builder 字彙與文法練習

A 看圖填空：依照圖片選出正確的單字。

1 Lungs help animals <u>breathe</u> air. 肺幫助動物呼吸。

2 Animals <u>need</u> food and water to live. 動物需要食物跟水才能生存。

3 Elephants are <u>huge</u> animals. 大象是巨大的動物。

4 Ants are <u>tiny</u>. 螞蟻很小。

B 牠們住在哪裡？圈出正確的單字，並填入空格中。

1 Squirrels live in _____**forest**_____. 松鼠住在森林裡。
   (forest) grassland

2 Lizards live in _____**desert**_____. 蜥蜴住在沙漠。
   ocean (desert)

3 Dolphins live in the _____**ocean**_____. 海豚在海洋中生活。
   (ocean) desert

4 Polar bears live at the _____**North Pole**_____. 北極熊住在北極。
   South Pole (North Pole)

Unit 07 A World of Insects

昆蟲世界

Reading Focus 閱讀焦點

- What are some insects? 昆蟲有哪些？
- How are insects alike? 昆蟲有哪些相同點？
- How many body parts does an insect have? 昆蟲的身體分成幾個部分？

Key Words 關鍵字彙

Insects
昆蟲

butterfly
蝴蝶

grasshopper
蚱蜢

bee
蜜蜂

beetle
甲蟲

ant
螞蟻

Insect Body Parts
昆蟲的身體部位

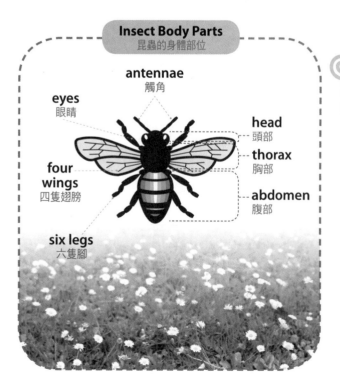

antennae 觸角

eyes 眼睛

head 頭部

thorax 胸部

abdomen 腹部

four wings 四隻翅膀

six legs 六隻腳

Power Verbs 核心動詞

come in
有……（接狀態）

Insects **come in** many shapes.
昆蟲有很多形狀。

take a look
看一看

Take a look at the ants.
看看這些螞蟻。

be divided into
被分成……

Insects **are divided into** three parts.
昆蟲被分成三個部分。

*divide 分類

touch
觸碰

Insects **touch** with their antennae.
昆蟲用牠們的觸角觸碰。

Word Families: Bees and Ants
相關字彙：蜜蜂與螞蟻

Kinds of Bees 蜜蜂的種類

queen bee
蜂后

male bee
雄蜂

female bee
= worker bee
母蜂＝工蜂

Kinds of Ants 螞蟻的種類

queen ant
蟻后

male ant
雄蟻

worker ant
工蟻

A World of Insects 昆蟲世界

看看這些圖片，
你能說出牠們的名字嗎？
螞蟻、蜜蜂、蝴蝶、甲蟲，
牠們都是昆蟲。

昆蟲有很多顏色、體型和大小，
每隻昆蟲的身體都有三個部分：
頭部、胸部和腹部。
而且昆蟲都擁有六隻腳，
有些昆蟲有翅膀可以飛行，有些則沒有。

螞蟻和蜜蜂都是昆蟲，
看看牠們。

牠們有幾隻腳？
牠們都有六隻腳，對吧？

牠們的身體都可以分為三個部分。

牠們的頭部有眼睛跟觸角，
觸角可以幫助昆蟲觸碰、嗅聞事物。

牠們的腳長在胸部的部分，
蜜蜂也長有翅膀，所以蜜蜂會飛。
大部分的螞蟻則沒有翅膀，
只有蟻后和雄蟻才有。

對大部分的昆蟲來說，身體最大的部位是腹部。

Check Understanding 文意測驗

1 下列圖片中分別是昆蟲身上的哪些部位？
a **wing(s)** 翅膀　　b **antenna(e)** 觸角

2 昆蟲有幾隻腳？ c
a 三隻　　b 四隻　　c 六隻

3 昆蟲的觸角長在哪裡？ a
a 頭部　　b 胸部　　c 腹部

4 蜜蜂有＿＿所以蜜蜂會飛。 c
a 觸角　　b 昆蟲　　c 翅膀

● 回答問題。

1 How do insects use their antennae? 昆蟲的觸角有什麼作用？
⇒ They use their antennae to **touch** and **smell**. 昆蟲用牠們的觸角去觸碰和嗅聞事物。

2 What is the largest part of most insects? 對大部分的昆蟲來說，身體上最大的部位是哪裡？
⇒ The largest part of most insects is the **abdomen**. 對大部分的昆蟲來說，身體最大的部位是腹部。

Vocabulary and Grammar Builder 字彙與文法練習

A 看圖填空：依照圖片選出正確的單字。
1 An insect's eyes are on its **head**. 昆蟲的眼睛長在頭部。
2 Insects **come in** many shapes and sizes. 昆蟲有很多體型和大小。
3 All insects have three **body parts**. 所有昆蟲的身體都有三個部分。
4 **Bees** have wings. 蜜蜂有翅膀。

B 哪一個部位？圈出正確的單字，並填入空格中。
1 All insects have a head, **thorax**, and abdomen. 所有的昆蟲都有頭部、胸部和腹部。
(thorax) wings
2 All insects have six **legs**. 所有的昆蟲都有六隻腳。
wings (legs)
3 Insects use their **antennae** to smell. 昆蟲用牠們的觸角嗅聞。
head (antennae)
4 Insects with **wings** can fly. 有翅膀的昆蟲可以飛。
(wings) abdomens

Unit 08 · What Are the Five Senses?

何謂五種官能？

Reading Focus 閱讀焦點

- What are the five senses? 何謂五種官能？
- What body parts do you use for each sense? 這些官能分別使用了身體的哪些部分去感覺？
- How do you use your senses? 你要如何使用你的官能？

Key Words 關鍵字彙

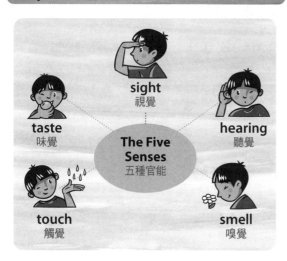

sight 視覺
hearing 聽覺
The Five Senses 五種官能
taste 味覺
touch 觸覺
smell 嗅覺

The Five Senses and Body Parts
五種官能對照身體部位

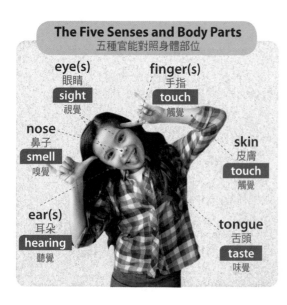

eye(s) 眼睛 · sight 視覺
finger(s) 手指 · touch 觸覺
nose 鼻子 · smell 嗅覺
skin 皮膚 · touch 觸覺
ear(s) 耳朵 · hearing 聽覺
tongue 舌頭 · taste 味覺

Power Verbs 核心動詞

see 看
She can **see** the flower.
她可以看見花。

hear 聽
He can **hear** the music.
他可以聽見音樂。

smell 嗅聞
It **smells** good.
聞起來味道很香。

taste 嚐
This cake **tastes** sweet.
這個蛋糕吃起來好甜。

touch 觸碰
Don't **touch** that hot stove.
不要觸碰熱燙的火爐。

Word Families: Senses 相關字彙：感覺

tastes 嚐
- bitter 苦的
- sour 酸的
- salty 鹹的
- sweet 甜的

feelings 感覺
- smooth 平滑的 ---- rough 粗糙的
- hot 熱的 ---- cold 冷的

sounds 聲音
- loud 大聲 ---- noisy 吵雜
- soft 舒服 ---- quiet 安靜

sight 視覺
- colorful 富有色彩的 · black and white 黑白的

smell 嗅覺
- fragrant 芳香的 · smelly 難聞的

118

What Are the Five Senses? 何謂五種官能？

早上時，瑪莉聽見她的鬧鐘響起，
她醒過來，環顧房間四周，
聞到了早餐的味道，
聞起來好香。
她馬上起床然後吃早餐，
早餐好好吃。

我們每天都在使用我們的官能，
人有五種官能，
分別是視覺、聽覺、嗅覺、味覺和觸覺。

不同的官能使用身體的不同部位去感受。

用眼睛去看，
當你看的時候，你會知道事物看起來怎麼樣。

用耳朵去聽，
當你聽的時候，你可以接收聲音並且了解意思。

用鼻子去聞，
氣味告訴你這東西聞起來怎麼樣。

用舌頭去嚐，
味道告訴你，食物是甜的、酸的、鹹的還是苦的。
巧克力吃起來是甜的，檸檬嚐起來是酸的。

用手指和皮膚去感覺，
觸覺告訴你某物是光滑的還是粗糙的，是熱的還是冷的。
泰迪熊摸起來是平滑的，火爐摸起來是熱的。

Check Understanding 文意測驗

1 下列圖片中的人們分別使用了哪些官能？

   a She is using her sense of **smell**. 她使用了嗅覺。
   b They are using their senses of **sight** and hearing. 他們使用了視覺和聽覺。

2 人有幾種官能？ **b**

   a 三種　　　　　　　b 五種　　　　　　　c 十種

3 當我們看見某物的時候，使用了哪一種官能？ **c**

   a 聽覺　　　　　　　b 味覺　　　　　　　c 視覺

4 你用_____去感覺東西。 **b**

   a 鼻子　　　　　　　b 手指　　　　　　　c 眼睛

● 回答問題。

1 What are the five senses? 何謂五種官能？
   ⇒ They are **sight**, **hearing**, **smell**, **taste**, and **touch**. 分別是視覺、聽覺、嗅覺、味覺和觸覺。

2 What are some tastes for foods? 食物的味道有哪些？
   ⇒ They are **sweet**, **sour**, **salty**, and **bitter**. 有甜的、酸的、鹹的和苦的。（spicy 辣的）

Vocabulary and Grammar Builder 字彙與文法練習

A 看圖填空：依照圖片選出正確的單字。

1 Mary **wakes up** early in the morning. 瑪莉早上很早就起床。
2 Lemon tastes **sour**. 檸檬吃起來是酸的。
3 When you hear, you **take in** sound. 當你聽的時候，你可以接收聲音。
4 A teddy bear feels **smooth**. 泰迪熊摸起來是平滑的。

B 單複數動詞：圈出正確的單字，並填入空格中。

1 The eyes ___**see**___ things. 眼睛看東西。
   (see) sees

2 The tongue ___**tastes**___ foods. 舌頭嚐食物。
   taste (tastes)

3 The ears ___**hear**___ sounds. 耳朵聽聲音。
   (hear) hears

4 The fingers ___**feel**___ different things. 手指感覺不同的事物。
   (feel) feels

119

The Little Red Hen

紅色小母雞

Reading Focus 閱讀焦點

- Which animals lived on the little red hen's farm? 紅色小母雞住的農場裡有些什麼動物？
- What sounds do those animals make? 這些動物的叫聲為何？
- Why did the little red hen eat the bread all by herself? 為什麼紅色小母雞自己把麵包全部吃掉？

Key Words 關鍵字彙

Who Is in the Story?
故事裡的角色

hen
母雞

pig
豬

duck
鴨子

cat
貓咪

Farm Crops
農場裡的穀物

wheat
小麥

corn
玉米

rice
稻穀

barley
大麥

Power Verbs 核心動詞

oink
齁齁（豬叫聲）

Pigs **oinked**.
豬齁齁地叫。

quack
呱呱（鴨叫聲）

Ducks **quacked**.
鴨子呱呱地叫。

meow
喵喵（貓叫聲）

Cats **meowed**.
貓喵喵地叫。

cluck
咕咕（雞叫聲）

Hens **clucked**.
母雞咕咕地叫。

Word Families: Past Tense
相關字彙：過去式

plant ⇨ planted
種植

grow ⇨ grew
成長

harvest ⇨ harvested
收成

cut ⇨ cut
收割

grind ⇨ ground
磨碎

bake ⇨ baked
烘焙

**From planting
to baking bread**
從種植到烤麵包的過程

The Little Red Hen 紅色小母雞

很久很久以前，有一隻紅色的小母雞，
她跟豬、鴨子還有貓咪住在一個農場裡。
她每天都勤奮地工作，
但是其他的動物們卻從來不幫忙。

有一天，紅色小母雞在花園裡發現了一些小麥的
穀粒。
小母雞心想：「我們可以種下這些小麥，讓它們
長大。」
所以她問：「誰想幫我種小麥？」
「我不要。」豬齁齁叫地回答。
「我不行。」鴨子呱呱叫地說。
「我不想。」貓咪喵喵叫地拒絕。
「好吧！我自己去種。」紅色小母雞咕咕叫地說。

到了夏天，這些小麥種子長大了，
然後，麥子變成了金黃色。
當這些麥子可以收成的時候，
紅色小母雞問道：「誰想要幫我割麥子？」
「我不要。」豬齁齁叫地回答。
「我不行。」鴨子呱呱叫地說。
「我不想。」貓咪喵喵叫地拒絕。
「好吧！我自己去割。」紅色小母雞咕咕叫地說。

當她收割完麥子之後，紅色小母雞又問：
「誰想要幫我磨麵粉？」
「我不要。」豬齁齁叫地回答。
「我不行。」鴨子呱呱叫地說。
「我不想。」貓咪喵喵叫地拒絕。
「好吧！我自己去磨。」紅色小母雞咕咕叫地說。

當她磨好麵粉之後，紅色小母雞再問：
「現在誰想幫我烤麵包？」
「我不要。」豬齁齁叫地回答。
「我不行。」鴨子呱呱叫地說。
「我不想。」貓咪喵喵叫地拒絕。
「好吧！我自己去烤。」紅色小母雞咕咕叫地說。

最後，當麵包出爐的時候，
看起來非常可口，而且香味四溢。

紅色小母雞問：
「現在誰想幫我吃麵包？」
「我要。」豬齁齁叫地回答。
「我可以。」鴨子呱呱叫地說。
「我也想。」貓咪喵喵叫地答應。
「不不不！你們不能，」紅色小母雞說：
「我自己種麥子，
我自己割麥子，
我自己磨麵粉，
而且我還自己烤麵包，
現在我也要『自己』吃麵包。」
然後就像她說的，
紅色小母雞自己吃掉了所有的麵包。

Check Understanding 文意測驗

1 下列圖片分別代表什麼意思？

　　a The little red hen is <u>planting</u> the wheat. 紅色小母正在雞種下麥子。
　　b The little red hen is <u>cutting</u> the wheat. 紅色小母雞正在收割麥子。

2 母雞怎麼叫？ **c**

　　a 喵喵　　　　　　　b 呱呱　　　　　　　c 咕咕

3 紅色小母雞用什麼方式將麥子變成麵粉？ **b**

　　a 種植　　　　　　　b 磨碎　　　　　　　c 烘烤

4 紅色小母雞將麵包放進_____裡烤。 **c**

　　a 農場　　　　　　　b 花園　　　　　　　c 烤爐

5 「all by myself」是什麼意思？ **a**

　　a 獨自（沒有別人的幫忙）b 合作　　　　　　c 分工做

6 將下列動物及牠們的叫聲連起來。

　　a 豬　　　　　　　　　　　　　喵喵
　　b 鴨子　　　　　　　　　　　　齁齁
　　c 貓　　　　　　　　　　　　　呱呱
　　d 母雞　　　　　　　　　　　　咕咕

● 回答問題。

1 Which animals lived on the little red hen's farm? 紅色小母雞住的農場裡有些什麼動物？
　⇨ A <u>pig</u>, a <u>duck</u>, and a <u>cat</u> lived on her farm. 豬、鴨子還有貓咪跟她住在一個農場裡。

2 Who ate the bread the little red hen baked? 誰吃了紅色小母雞烤的麵包？
　⇨ The little red hen ate the bread <u>all</u> <u>by</u> <u>herself</u>. 紅色小母雞自己吃了所有的麵包。

Vocabulary and Grammar Builder 字彙與文法練習

Ⓐ 看圖填空：依照圖片選出正確的單字。

1 She <u>found</u> some grains of wheat. 她發現了一些小麥的穀粒。

2 She <u>harvested</u> the wheat. 她收割麥子。

3 She <u>planted</u> the seeds of wheat. 她種下小麥的穀粒。

4 She used <u>flour</u> to make the bread. 她用麵粉做麵包。

Ⓑ 動詞過去式：圈出正確的單字，並填入空格中。

1 The little red hen ____**planted**____ the seeds. (plant) 紅色小母雞種下麥子。
　　plantted　(planted)

2 The little red hen ____**cut**____ the wheat. (cut) 紅色小母雞收割麥子。
　　(cut)　cutted

3 The little red hen ____**ground**____ the wheat into flour. (grind)
　　(ground)　grounded
　　紅色小母雞把麥子磨成麵粉。

4 The little red hen ____**baked**____ the bread. (bake) 紅色小母雞烤麵包。
　　bakeed　(baked)

Unit 10

Numbers from 1 to 10

數字 1 到 10

Reading Focus 閱讀焦點

• What are the numbers from 1 to 10? 1 到 10 的數字有哪些？

• Which number comes after 1? 1 之後是哪個數字呢？

• What numbers are less than 5? 哪些數字比 5 小？

Key Words 關鍵字彙

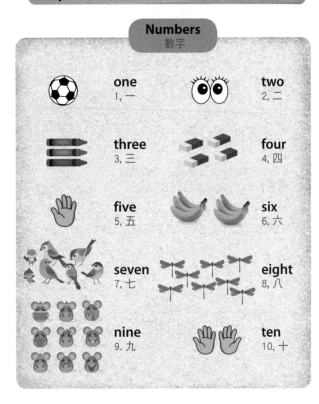

Numbers
數字

one
1, 一

two
2, 二

three
3, 三

four
4, 四

five
5, 五

six
6, 六

seven
7, 七

eight
8, 八

nine
9, 九

ten
10, 十

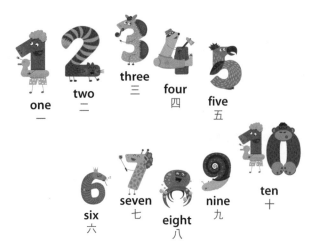

one
一

two
二

three
三

four
四

five
五

six
六

seven
七

eight
八

nine
九

ten
十

Power Verbs 核心動詞

count
計算

Let's **count** the candles.
讓我們數一數有幾根蠟燭。

say aloud
大聲說（唸）

Let's **say** the numbers **aloud**.
讓我們大聲的唸出這些數字。

Word Families 相關字彙

come before
在⋯⋯之前

3 **comes before** 4.
3 在 4 之前。

come after
在⋯⋯之後

4 **comes after** 3.
4 在 3 之後。

less than
比⋯⋯少

One is **less than** two. (1 < 2)
一比二少。

more than
比⋯⋯多

Two is **more than** one. (2 > 1)
二比一多。

left hand 左手　right hand 右手

hand
手

You have **two hands**.
你有兩隻手。

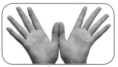

finger
手指

You have **ten fingers**.
你有十根手指。

124

Numbers from 1 to 10 數字 1 到 10

看看這個生日蛋糕，上面插了幾支蠟燭呢？
一、二、三、四、五、
六、七、八、九、十。
上面有十支蠟燭，傑克十歲了。

當我們計算的時候，就會用到數字。
有一隻狗。有三隻貓。

這裡有數字 1 到 10，
讓我們一個一個大聲的唸出來。

1 之後是 2，2 之後是 3，
2 之前是 1，3 之前是 2。

現在，回答下面的問題。

你有幾個鼻子？一個！你有一個鼻子。
你有幾個眼睛？兩個！你有兩個眼睛。

一比二少，二比一多。

你的左手有幾根手指？
五根！你的左手有五根手指。

你的右手有幾根手指？
五根！你的右手有五根手指。

你的兩隻手共有幾根手指？
十根！你的兩隻手共有十根手指。

五比十小，十比五大。

Check Understanding 文意測驗

1 下列圖片中的物品分別有多少？
   a 6 / six 六   **b 9 / nine** 九

2 你有幾個眼睛？ **b**
   a 一個   b 兩個   c 三個

3 7 之前是哪一個數字？ **c**
   a 7   b 5   c 6

4 8 比 9 _____。 **a**
   a 少   b 多   c 之前

● 回答問題。

1 What are the numbers from 1 to 5? 1 到 5 的數字有哪些？
   ⇨ They are **one**, **two**, **three**, **four**, and **five**. 有一、二、三、四、五。

2 What are the numbers from 6 to 10? 6 到 10 的數字有哪些？
   ⇨ They are **six**, **seven**, **eight**, **nine**, and **ten**. 有六、七、八、九、十。

Vocabulary and Grammar Builder 字彙與文法練習

Ⓐ 看圖填空：依照圖片選出正確的單字。
   1 **How many** ears do you have? 你有幾個耳朵？
   2 5 comes **before** 6. 5 在 6 的前面。
   3 There are **seven** cats. 有七隻貓。
   4 8 is **more than** 5. 8 比 5 多。

Ⓑ 多還是少？圈出正確的單字，並填入空格中。
   1 One is ____**less**____ than two. 一比二少。
      more (less)
   2 Eight is ____**more**____ than four. 八比四多。
      (more) less
   3 Seven comes ____**after**____ three. 七在三之後。
      before (after)
   4 Nine comes ____**before**____ ten. 九在十之前。
      (before) after

125

Lines and Shapes
線條和形狀

Reading Focus 閱讀焦點

- What are some lines? 線條有哪些？
- What are some shapes? 形狀有哪些？
- How can you make shapes? 如何畫出形狀？

Key Words 關鍵字彙

Types of Lines 線條的種類

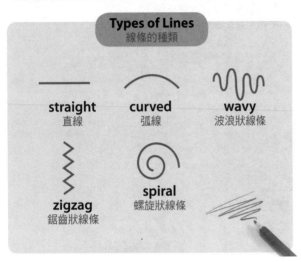

straight 直線　　**curved** 弧線　　**wavy** 波浪狀線條

zigzag 鋸齒狀線條　　**spiral** 螺旋狀線條

Shapes 形狀

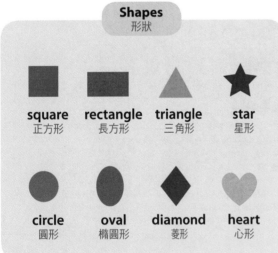

square 正方形　　**rectangle** 長方形　　**triangle** 三角形　　**star** 星形

circle 圓形　　**oval** 橢圓形　　**diamond** 菱形　　**heart** 心形

Power Verbs 核心動詞

draw 畫（畫、圖）
Draw a line. 畫一條線。

join 組合
You can **join** two lines together. 可以把兩條線組合在一起。

be made of 由……組成
Shapes **are made of** lines. 形狀由線條所組成。

name 叫出（名字）
Can you **name** these shapes? 你能說出這些是什麼形狀嗎？

Word Families 相關字彙

thick 粗的　　**thin** 細的　　**round** 圓的

look alike 看起來很像
They **look alike.** 它們看起來很像。

look different 看起來不同
They **look different.** 它們看起來很不同。

pencil 鉛筆　　**colored pencil** 色鉛筆　　**crayon** 蠟筆　　**marker** 麥克筆

drawing materials 繪畫工具

Lines and Shapes 線條和形狀

瑪莉正在畫一張房子的圖，
你能看見畫裡有這些線條嗎？ ─ ｜ ⌇

我們用線條來畫出圖畫，
如果你想畫出香蕉，可以先畫出這樣的弧線。 ⌒

這裡有很多種線條：
⌒ ─ ⌇ ⌇ ⊚

線條可以細，也可以粗，
用削尖的鉛筆可以畫出細的線條，
用蠟筆可以畫出粗的線條。

當線條集合在一起，就會組合出形狀。

你能說出這些是什麼形狀嗎？
它們分別是圓形、三角形、正方形和長方形。
○ △ □ ▭

圓形是圓圓的，由弧線所組成。
三角形、正方形和長方形，是由直線所組成。

正方形和長方形長得很像，
圓形和三角形看起來就不一樣。

這裡有四種形狀：
菱形、星形、心形和橢圓形。 ◇ ☆ ♡ ◯

在下列圖片中你可以找到哪些線條？
螺旋狀線條、弧線、鋸齒狀線條

Check Understanding 文意測驗

1　在下列圖片中你可以找到哪些線條？
　　a curved line(s) 弧線　**b** spiral line 螺旋狀線條

2　鉛筆可以畫出什麼樣的線條？　**a**
　　a 細的線條　　　**b** 粗的線條　　　**c** 小的線條

3　＿＿＿＿和長方形看起來長得很像。　**b**
　　a 圓形　　　　　**b** 正方形　　　　**c** 三角形

4　當線條集合在一起，就會組合出＿＿＿＿。　**b**
　　a 圓形　　　　　**b** 形狀　　　　　**c** 心形

● 回答問題。

1　What are some different types of lines? 線條有哪些不同的種類？
　　⇨ There are **curved**, **straight**, **wavy**, **zigzag**, and **spiral** lines.
　　有弧線、直線、波浪狀線條、鋸齒狀線條和螺旋狀線條。

2　How do a circle and a rectangle look? 圓形跟長方形看起來怎麼樣？
　　⇨ A circle and a rectangle look **different**. 圓形跟長方形看起來很不一樣。

Vocabulary and Grammar Builder 字彙與文法練習

A 看圖填空：依照圖片選出正確的單字。

1　He is **drawing** a picture. 他正在畫圖。
2　A crayon makes a **thick line**. 蠟筆可以畫出粗的線條。
3　A circle is **round**. 圓形是圓圓的。
4　A square is **made of** four straight lines. 正方形是由四條直線所組成。

B 相似或不同：圈出正確的單字，並填入空格中。

1　A square and a rectangle look ＿＿**alike**＿＿. 正方形和長方形看起來很像。
　　(alike) different
2　A triangle and a circle look ＿＿**different**＿＿. 三角形跟圓形看起來很不一樣。
　　alike (different)
3　A zigzag line and a straight line look ＿＿**different**＿＿. 鋸齒狀線條和直線看起來很不一樣。
　　alike (different)
4　A circle and an oval look ＿＿**alike**＿＿. 圓形和橢圓形看起來很像。
　　(alike) different

127

Let's Beat the Drum

大家一起來打鼓

Reading Focus 閱讀焦點

- What are some musical instruments? 樂器有哪些？
- Can you play any musical instruments? 你會演奏哪些樂器嗎？
- How do you play those musical instruments? 你都怎麼演奏這些樂器？

Key Words 關鍵字彙

Musical Instruments
樂器

piano
鋼琴

violin
小提琴

drumstick
鼓棒

stick
鐵棒

drum
鼓

triangle
三角鐵

tambourine
鈴鼓

stick
琴棒

xylophone
木琴

cymbals
鐃鈸

castanets
響板

Power Verbs 核心動詞

play
演奏（樂器）

She can **play** the piano.
她會彈鋼琴。

hit
敲擊

Hit the triangle with a stick.
用鐵棒敲擊三角鐵。

beat
敲打

You **beat** the drum.
打鼓。

tap
輕輕敲擊

You **tap** the xylophone.
輕輕敲擊木琴。

shake
搖晃

You **shake** the tambourine.
搖晃鈴鼓。

bang
撞擊

You **bang** the cymbals.
撞擊鐃鈸。

click
輕點

You **click** the castanets.
輕點響板。

Let's Beat the Drum 大家一起來打鼓

你喜歡音樂嗎？
你喜歡唱歌跳舞嗎？
還是喜歡演奏樂器呢？

這裡有很多種樂器，
讓我們一起認識一些有趣的樂器吧！
這些是什麼樂器呢？

沒錯！它們分別是鼓、三角鐵和木琴，
通稱為打擊樂器。

打擊樂器演奏起來很有趣，
你可以用手或是棒子敲打它們。

你可以舉出其他的打擊樂器嗎？
你覺得鈴鼓算是嗎？
鐃鈸呢？還是響板？
通通都對！它們都是打擊樂器家族的一員。

大家一起演奏它們！
鼓有鼓棒，
你要用鼓棒打鼓。
而木琴也有琴棒，
你可以用琴棒輕輕敲擊木琴。

你可以用手搖晃鈴鼓，
鐃鈸也是用手直接撞擊演奏。
而響板只需要用你的手指輕點就能演奏。

Check Understanding 文意測驗

1 下列圖片中分別是什麼樂器？
   a **piano** 鋼琴   **b** **xylophone** 木琴   **c** **triangle** 三角鐵   **d** **cymbals** 鐃鈸

2 要用什麼打鼓？ **b**
   a 鈴鼓   **b** 鼓棒   **c** 三角鐵

3 木琴屬於哪種樂器？ **a**
   a 打擊樂器   **b** 鍵盤樂器   **c** 好玩的樂器

4 你用你的手指_____來演奏響板。 **c**
   a 撞擊   **b** 搖晃   **c** 輕點

● 回答問題。

1 How do you play the cymbals? 鐃鈸怎麼演奏？
   ⇨ You **bang** the cymbals with your hands. 用手撞擊鐃鈸就能演奏。

2 How do you play the tambourine? 鈴鼓怎麼演奏？
   ⇨ You **shake** the tambourine with your hands. 用手搖晃鈴鼓就能演奏。

Vocabulary and Grammar Builder 字彙與文法練習

A 看圖填空：依照圖片選出正確的單字。

1 The boy beats the **drum**. 那個男孩在打鼓。

2 She **hits** the triangle. 她在敲擊三角鐵。

3 **Percussion** instruments are fun to play. 打擊樂器演奏起來很有趣。

4 The xylophone has a **stick**. 木琴有琴棒。

B 演奏動作：圈出正確的單字，並填入空格中。

1 You ___**play**___ the piano with your fingers. 用手指彈奏鋼琴。
   shake (play)

2 You ___**tap**___ the xylophone with a stick. 用琴棒輕輕敲擊木琴。
   click (tap)

3 You ___**bang**___ the cymbals. 撞擊鐃鈸。
   (bang) shake

4 You ___**shake**___ the tambourine. 搖晃鈴鼓。
   click (shake)

129

A 看圖填空：依照圖片選出正確的單字。

1 Flowers __bloom__ in spring. 花在春天綻放。

2 An island is __surrounded__ by water. 島嶼四周被水環繞。

3 __Firefighters__ put out dangerous fire. 消防員撲滅危險的惡火。

4 A tanker truck __carries__ oil and gas. 油罐車載運石油和汽油。

B 圈出正確的單字，並將答案填入空格中。

1 Fall comes ___after___ summer. 秋天在夏天之後到來。
before (after)

2 A waiter ___serves___ food at a restaurant. 服務生在餐廳裡為客人上菜。
serve (serves)

3 A valley is the ___low land___ between mountains. 山谷是高山之間的低地。
high land (low land)

4 A ___ship___ moves on the water. 船在水面上移動。
jet (ship)

C 選出正確的單字填入空格中。

1 Leaves __change colors__ in fall. 葉子在秋天改變顏色。

2 __Winter__ comes before spring. 冬天在春天之前到來。

3 Weather changes from __season__ to season. 天氣隨著季節更替而改變。

4 Fall is __warmer__ than winter. 秋天比冬天溫暖。

5 Earth is __made up of__ land and water. 地球由陸地和水所組成。

6 Earth has different __kinds of__ land. 地球上有很多不同的地形。

7 __Flat land__ is called a plain. 我們稱平坦的土地為平原。

8 Rivers __flow into__ oceans. 河流滾滾流進海洋。

D 選出正確的單字填入空格中。

1 A __job__ is the work people do. 職業是人們做的工作。

2 Most people have jobs to __earn__ money. 大部分的人為了賺錢而工作。

3 Some people __work for__ the community. 有些人為社會大眾工作。

4 Some volunteers __serve__ food to homeless people. 有些義工分送食物給無家可歸的人。

5 __Transportation__ moves people or things from one place to another.
交通工具將人們或物品從某個地方運送到其他地方。

6 Jenny __rides__ her bike to school. 珍妮騎腳踏車去上學。

7 Some people __drive__ their cars to work. 有些人自己開車去上班。

8 Airplanes and helicopters move __in the air__. 飛機和直升機在空中翱翔。

Ⓐ 看圖填空：依照圖片選出正確的單字。

1 These are both <u>roots</u>. 這些都是根部。

2 <u>Gills</u> help fish breathe in water. 鰓幫助魚在水中呼吸。

3 All insects have three <u>body parts</u>. 所有昆蟲的身體都有三個部分。

4 This cake <u>tastes</u> delicious. 這個蛋糕嚐起來很好吃。

Ⓑ 圈出正確的單字，並將答案填入空格中。

1 _____<u>Oranges</u>_____ are delicious fruits. 柳橙是可口的水果。
An orange (Oranges)

2 Penguins live at the _____<u>South Pole</u>_____. 企鵝住在南極。
(South Pole) North Pole

3 All insects have a head, _____<u>thorax</u>_____, and abdomen. 所有的昆蟲都有頭部、胸部和腹部。
(thorax) wings

4 This flower _____<u>smells</u>_____ good. 這朵花聞起來很香。
smell (smells)

Ⓒ 選出正確的單字填入空格中。

1 Grass, vegetables, and trees are all <u>plants</u>. 青草、蔬菜和樹木都是植物。

2 We eat leaves, such as <u>lettuce</u> and cabbage. 我們會吃葉子，像是萵苣和甘藍菜。

3 Apples and pears are <u>fruits</u> we eat. 蘋果和梨子是我們會吃的果實。

4 Corn, rice, and peanuts are all the <u>seeds</u> of the plants. 玉米、稻穀和花生都是植物的種子。

5 <u>Lungs</u> help animals breathe air. 肺幫助動物呼吸空氣。

6 Snakes and lizards live in <u>deserts</u>. 蛇和蜥蜴住在沙漠裡。

7 Giraffes, elephants, and lions live in <u>grasslands</u>. 長頸鹿、大象和獅子住在大草原上。

8 Sharks, whales, and dolphins live in the <u>ocean</u>. 鯊魚、鯨魚和海豚都在海洋中生活。

Ⓓ 選出正確的單字填入空格中。

1 <u>Insects</u> have three body parts and six legs. 昆蟲有三個身體部位和六隻腳。

2 Insects <u>come in</u> many colors, shapes, and sizes. 昆蟲有很多顏色、體型和大小。

3 The <u>antennas</u> help insects touch and smell. 昆蟲使用觸角觸碰和嗅聞事物。

4 Insects' legs are on their <u>thoraxes</u>. 昆蟲的腳長在胸部的部分。

5 The five senses are <u>sight</u>, hearing, smell, taste, and touch. 五種官能就是視覺、聽覺、嗅覺、味覺和觸覺。

6 When you <u>see</u>, you know how things look. 當你看的時候，你會知道事物看起來怎麼樣。

7 You use your <u>tongue</u> to taste. 你使用舌頭去品嚐。

8 <u>Touch</u> tells you if things are smooth, rough, hot, or cold.
觸覺告訴你某物是光滑的還是粗糙的，是熱的還是冷的。

Ⓐ 看圖填空：依照圖片選出正確的單字。

1 The little red hen **harvested** the wheat. 紅色小母雞收割麥子。

2 8 comes **after** 7. 8 在 7 之後。

3 A circle is **made of** a curved line. 圓形是由弧線所組成。

4 The drum has a **drumstick**. 鼓有鼓棒。

Ⓑ 圈出正確的單字，並將答案填入空格中。

1 The little red hen _____**ground**_____ the wheat into flour. 紅色小母雞把麥子磨成麵粉。
(ground) grounded

2 Six is _____**more**_____ than four. 六比四多。
(more) less

3 A square and a rectangle look _____**alike**_____. 正方形和長方形看起來很像。
(alike) different

4 You _____**click**_____ the castanets with your fingers. 用手指輕點響板就能演奏。
shake (click)

Ⓒ 選出正確的單字填入空格中。

1 A little red hen lived on a **farm** with a pig, a duck, and a cat.
紅色的小母雞跟豬、鴨子還有貓咪住在一個農場裡。

2 One day, the little red hen found some **grains** of wheat.
有一天，紅色小母雞發現了一些小麥的穀粒。

3 The little red hen ground the wheat into **flour**. 紅色小母雞把麥子磨成麵粉。

4 The little red hen ate the bread all **by herself**. 紅色小母雞自己吃掉了所有的麵包。

5 We use numbers when we **count**. 當我們計算的時候，就會用到數字。

6 You have **ten** fingers on both hands. 你的兩隻手共有十根手指。

7 Two is **less** than three. 二比三少。

8 How **many** eyes do you have? 你有幾個眼睛？

Ⓓ 選出正確的單字填入空格中。

1 We use lines when we **draw** pictures. 當我們畫圖的時候，我們用線條來畫出圖畫。

2 When lines join together, they make **shapes**. 當線條集合在一起，就會組合出形狀。

3 A circle and an oval look **alike**. 圓形和橢圓形看起來很像。

4 A circle and a triangle look **different**. 圓形和三角形看起來很不一樣。

5 Drums and triangles are **percussion** instruments. 鼓和三角鐵都是打擊樂器。

6 You hit percussion instruments with your hands or a **stick**. 你可以用手或棒子敲打打擊樂器。

7 You **tap** the xylophone with a stick. 用琴棒輕輕敲擊木琴。

8 You **shake** the tambourine with your hands. 用手搖晃鈴鼓。

Authors

Michael A. Putlack

Michael A. Putlack graduated from Tufts University in Medford, Massachusetts, USA, where he got his B.A. in History and English and his M.A. in History. He has written a number of books for children, teenagers, and adults.

e-Creative Contents

A creative group that develops English contents and products for ESL and EFL students.

FÜN學
美國各學科初級課本 ①
新生入門英語閱讀

作 者	Michael A. Putlack & e-Creative Contents
譯 者	陸葵珍
編 輯	賴祖兒／陸葵珍
主 編	丁宥暄
內文排版	謝青秀／林書玉
封面設計	林書玉
製程管理	洪巧玲
發行人	黃朝萍
出版者	寂天文化事業股份有限公司
電 話	+886-(0)2-2365-9739
傳 真	+886-(0)2-2365-9835
網 址	www.icosmos.com.tw
讀者服務	onlineservice@icosmos.com.tw
出版日期	2023 年 11 月 二版再刷（寂天雲隨身聽 APP 版）(080204)

國家圖書館出版品預行編目資料

Fun學美國各學科初級課本 1：新生入門英語閱讀
(寂天隨身聽APP版) / Michael A. Putlack,
e-Creative Contents著.
-- 二版. -- 臺北市：寂天文化, 2021.08-
　冊；　公分
ISBN 978-626-300-051-3 (第1冊：菊8K平裝)

1.英語 2.讀本

805.18   110013028

郵撥帳號 1998620-0 寂天文化事業股份有限公司
訂書金額未滿 1000 元，請外加運費 100 元。
〔若有破損，請寄回更換，謝謝。〕

FÜN學

美國各學科初級課本

新生入門英語閱讀 二版

AMERICAN
SCHOOL
TEXTBOOK

Reading
Key BASIC

WORKBOOK
練習本

Seasons and Weather

A Write the meaning of each word and phrase in Chinese.

1 look _____

2 outside _____

3 sunny _____

4 cloudy _____

5 weather _____

6 change _____

7 from day to day _____

8 can be _____

9 rainy _____

10 snowy _____

11 season _____

12 from season to season _____

13 year _____

14 four seasons _____

15 spring _____

16 summer _____

17 fall _____

18 winter _____

19 warm _____

20 flower _____

21 begin to _____

22 bloom _____

23 come after _____

24 hot _____

25 the warmest _____

26 cooler _____

27 than _____

28 leaf _____

29 leaves _____

30 change colors _____

31 cold _____

32 the coldest _____

B Choose the word that best completes each sentence.

snowy	changes	warmer	seasons

1 Weather _____ from day to day.

2 A year has four _____.

3 Summer is _____ than spring.

4 Winter is very cold and _____.

▶ B, C大題解答請參照主冊課文
A大題解答請參照 Word List（主冊P. 93）

3

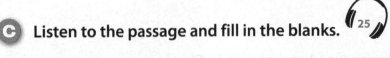

C **Listen to the passage and fill in the blanks.** 25

Look _____.

Is it sunny? Is it _____?

Weather changes from _____ to day.

It can be _____.

It can be _____.

It can be _____ or snowy.

Weather changes from _____ to season, too.

A year has _____ seasons.

They are spring, summer, fall, and _____.

Spring is _____.

Flowers begin to bloom in _____.

Summer comes _____ spring.

Summer is very _____ and sunny.

It is the _____ season.

_____ comes after summer.

Fall is _____ than summer.

Leaves change _____ in fall.

_____ comes after fall.

Winter is very _____ and snowy.

It is the _____ season.

A Write the meaning of each word and phrase in Chinese.

1 Earth _____
2 be made up of _____
3 land _____
4 water _____
5 picture _____
6 tell _____
7 which part _____
8 kind _____
9 different kinds of _____
10 mountain _____
11 the highest _____
12 form _____
13 form of land _____
14 hill _____
15 lower than _____
16 valley _____
17 low _____
18 between _____
19 usually _____
20 narrow _____

21 flat _____
22 be called _____
23 plain _____
24 be good for _____
25 farming _____
26 desert _____
27 dry _____
28 very little rain _____
29 island _____
30 be surrounded by _____
31 ocean _____
32 the largest _____
33 body of water _____
34 cover _____
35 much of _____
36 lake _____
37 large _____
38 river _____
39 long _____
40 flow into _____

B Choose the word that best completes each sentence.

river	made up of	plain

1 Earth is _____ land and water.

2 A _____ is good for farming.

3 A _____ flows into an ocean.

Listen to the passage and fill in the blanks. 26

Earth is _____ _____ _____ land and water.

This is a _____ of Earth.

Can you tell _____ part is land?

Which part is _____?

Earth has different _____ _____ land.

A _____ is the highest form of land.

A hill is _____ than a mountain.

A valley is the low land _____ mountains.

A valley is usually _____.

Some land is _____.

Flat land is _____ a plain.

A _____ is good for farming.

A desert is a _____ land.

A _____ has very little rain.

An island is _____ by water.

Earth has _____ kinds of water.

An _____ is the largest body of water.

Oceans cover _____ our Earth.

A _____ is a large body of water.

It is surrounded by _____.

A river is a long _____ of water.

It _____ into an ocean.

Daily Test 03 — **Many Jobs**

A Write the meaning of each word and phrase in Chinese.

1	my home	_____	22	waiter	_____
2	lots of	_____	23	serve	_____
3	job	_____	24	restaurant	_____
4	help	_____	25	doctor	_____
5	feed	_____	26	be sick	_____
6	water	_____	27	work for	_____
7	plant	_____	28	community	_____
8	my mom	_____	29	firefighter	_____
9	cook	_____	30	put out	_____
10	dinner	_____	31	dangerous	_____
11	work	_____	32	fire	_____
12	earn	_____	33	police officer	_____
13	there are	_____	34	safety	_____
14	many kinds of	_____	35	volunteer	_____
15	farmer	_____	36	for free	_____
16	grow	_____	37	homeless	_____
17	fruit	_____	38	hospital	_____
18	vegetable	_____	39	all kinds of	_____
19	worker	_____	40	important	_____
20	factory	_____	41	what kind of	_____
21	service job	_____	42	would like to	_____

B Choose the word that best completes each sentence.

> earn · community volunteers

1 Most people have jobs to _____ money.

2 Police officers work for the safety of the _____.

3 _____ work for free to help others.

Listen to the passage and fill in the blanks. 27

My name is _____. This is my _____.

I do lots of _____ to help at home.

I _____ my dog. I _____ the plants.

I help my mom _____ dinner.

What are your jobs _____ _____?

A job is the _____ people do.

Most people have jobs to _____ money.

There are many _____ _____ jobs.

Farmers grow _____ and vegetables.

Some workers work in _____.

Some people have _____ jobs.

A waiter _____ food at a restaurant.

A doctor helps people who are _____.

Some people work for the _____.

_____ put out dangerous fires.

Police officers work for the _____ of the community.

Some _____ are volunteers.

_____ work for free to help others.

Some volunteers serve food to _____ people.

Some volunteers work at _____.

All kinds of work are _____.

What kind of work _____ you like to do?

8

A Write the meaning of each word and phrase in Chinese.

1 student _____

2 ride _____

3 bike _____

4 school _____

5 sometimes _____

6 take _____

7 school bus _____

8 transportation _____

9 move _____

10 thing _____

11 from one place to another

_____

12 drive _____

13 work _____

14 subway _____

15 a lot of _____

16 at one time _____

17 delivery truck _____

18 deliver _____

19 tanker truck _____

20 carry _____

21 oil _____

22 gas _____

23 train _____

24 airplane _____

25 helicopter _____

26 in the air _____

27 fly _____

28 around the world _____

29 transport _____

30 goods _____

31 travel _____

32 on the water _____

33 ship _____

34 ferry _____

B Choose the word that best completes each sentence.

carries	transportation	transport

1 _____ moves people or things from one place to another.

2 A tanker truck _____ oil and gas.

3 Many ships and ferries _____ people and goods.

C **Listen to the passage and fill in the blanks.** 28

Jenny is a _____.

She _____ her bike to school.

Sometimes she _____ the school bus, too.

The _____ and the school bus are her transportation.

Transportation _____ people or things from one place to another.

What kinds of _____ do you use?

Some people _____ their cars to work.

Some people take the _____ to work.

Some people take _____ to work.

Some kinds of transportation move a lot of things ____ _____ _____.

A delivery truck _____ things to people.

A _____ truck carries oil and gas.

A train can also carry a lot of _____ at one time.

Airplanes and _____ move in the air.

Airplanes can _____ around the world to transport people and goods.

People also _____ on the water.

Many ships and _____ transport people and goods.

10

A Write the meaning of each word and phrase in Chinese.

1	garden	18	seed
2	grow	19	radish
3	plant	20	onion
4	different	21	carrot
5	many different kinds of	22	celery
6	big	23	such as
7	small	24	lettuce
8	grass	25	cabbage
9	vegetable	26	broccoli
10	tree	27	cauliflower
11	part	28	apple
12	root	29	pear
13	stem	30	strawberry
14	leaf	31	sometimes
15	flower	32	corn
16	fruit	33	rice
17	hold	34	peanut

B Choose the word that best completes each sentence.

fruits	stems	plants	roots

1   Grass, vegetables, and trees are all _____.

2   Most plants have roots, _____, and leaves.

3   Radishes, onions, and carrots are the _____ of plants.

4   Apples, pears, and strawberries are _____ we eat.

11

C **Listen to the passage and fill in the blanks.** 🎧 29

I am Scott. And this is my _____.

I _____ many plants here.

There are many _____ kinds of plants.

Plants can be _____ or _____.

Grass, _____, and trees are all plants.

Plants have different _____.

Most _____ have roots, stems, and leaves.

Many plants have _____, too.

The flowers make _____.

The fruits hold _____.

We can eat many _____ _____.

We eat _____.

Radishes, onions, and _____ are the roots of plants.

We eat _____.

_____ is the stem of a plant.

We eat _____, such as lettuce and cabbage.

We eat flowers, such as _____ and cauliflower.

We eat the _____ of many plants, too.

Apples, pears, and _____ are fruits we eat.

_____ we eat the seeds of plants, too.

Corn, rice, and _____ are all the seeds of plants.

12

A **Write the meaning of each word and phrase in Chinese.**

1	favorite	_____	20 place	_____
2	animal	_____	21 forest	_____
3	like	_____	22 bear	_____
4	dog	_____	23 squirrel	_____
5	cat	_____	24 deer	_____
6	tiny	_____	25 grassland	_____
7	like	_____	26 giraffe	_____
8	ant	_____	27 lion	_____
9	huge	_____	28 snake	_____
10	elephant	_____	29 lizard	_____
11	need	_____	30 desert	_____
12	food	_____	31 a few	_____
13	live	_____	32 polar bear	_____
14	air	_____	33 the North Pole	_____
15	lung	_____	34 penguin	_____
16	help	_____	35 the South Pole	_____
17	breathe	_____	36 shark	_____
18	gill	_____	37 whale	_____
19	fish	_____	38 dolphin	_____

B **Choose the word that best completes each sentence.**

need	ocean	breathe	grasslands

1 Animals _____ food and water to live.

2 Lungs help animals _____ air.

3 Giraffes, elephants, and lions live in _____.

4 Sharks, whales, and dolphins live in the _____.

What's your _____ animal?

Do you like _____? Do you like _____?

There are many different _____ _____ animals.

Some animals are _____ like ants.

Some animals are _____ like elephants.

Animals _____ food and water to live.

Some animals eat _____ .

Some animals _____ other animals.

Animals need _____, too.

Lungs help animals _____ air.

_____ help fish breathe in water.

All animals need _____ to live, too.

Animals _____ _____ different places.

Many animals live in _____ .

_____, squirrels, and deer live in forests.

Other animals live in _____ .

Giraffes, _____, and lions live in grasslands.

Some animals, like snakes and _____, live in deserts.

_____ animals live in very cold places.

Polar bears live at the _____ _____ .

Penguins live at the _____ _____ .

And _____ live in water.

Sharks, whales, and _____ live in the ocean.

14

A **Write the meaning of each word and phrase in Chinese.**

1 look at _____
2 picture _____
3 name _____
4 each of _____
5 ant _____
6 honeybee _____
7 butterfly _____
8 beetle _____
9 insect _____
10 come in _____
11 color _____
12 shape _____
13 size _____
14 body part _____
15 head _____
16 thorax _____

17 abdomen _____
18 leg _____
19 wing _____
20 fly _____
21 bee _____
22 both _____
23 take a look at _____
24 close _____
25 divide _____
26 be divided into _____
27 antenna _____
28 touch _____
29 smell _____
30 only _____
31 queen ant _____
32 male ant _____

B **Choose the word that best completes each sentence.**

insects	wings	thorax	antennae

1 _____ come in many colors, shapes, and sizes.

2 Every insect has three body parts: a head, _____, and abdomen.

3 The _____ help insects touch and smell.

4 Bees have _____ so they can fly.

15

C Listen to the passage and fill in the blanks. 31

Look at the _____.

Can you name _____ _____ them?

ant   honeybee   _____   beetle

They are all _____.

Insects _____ _____ many colors, shapes, and sizes.

But every insect has three body parts: a head, thorax, and _____.

And insects all have six _____.

Some insects have _____ and can fly. Some have _____ wings.

Ants and _____ are both insects.

Take a _____ _____ them.

How many legs do they _____?

They all have six legs, _____?

Their bodies are _____ into three parts.

Their eyes and antennae are on their _____.

The _____ help insects touch and smell.

Their legs are on their _____.

Bees have wings there, _____. So bees can _____.

But most _____ do not have wings.

Only queen ants and _____ ants have wings.

The abdomen is the _____ part of most insects.

16

What Are the Five Senses?

A Write the meaning of each word and phrase in Chinese.

1 hear _____
2 alarm clock _____
3 ring _____
4 in the morning _____
5 wake up _____
6 look around _____
7 smell _____
8 breakfast _____
9 get up _____
10 taste _____
11 use _____
12 sense _____
13 every day _____
14 five senses _____
15 sight _____
16 hearing _____
17 smell _____
18 taste _____
19 touch _____
20 see _____
21 know _____

22 look _____
23 hear _____
24 take in _____
25 sound _____
26 understand _____
27 tell _____
28 tongue _____
29 if _____
30 sweet _____
31 sour _____
32 salty _____
33 bitter _____
34 chocolate _____
35 lemon _____
36 finger _____
37 skin _____
38 feel _____
39 smooth _____
40 rough _____
41 teddy bear _____
42 stove _____

B Choose the word that best completes each sentence.

taste	five senses	fingers	touch

1 The _____ are sight, hearing, smell, taste, and touch.

2 You use your _____ and skin to feel.

3 You use your tongue to _____.

4 _____ tells you if things are smooth, rough, hot, or cold.

Listen to the passage and fill in the blanks. 32

Mary hears her alarm clock _____ in the morning.

She _____ _____ and looks around her room.

She smells _____.

It _____ good.

She _____ _____ and eats her breakfast.

It _____ good.

We use our _____ every day.

_____ have five senses.

They are _____, hearing, smell, taste, and touch.

You use different body parts for _____ senses.

You use your _____ to see.

When you see, you know how things _____.

You use your _____ to hear.

When you hear, you _____ _____ sound and understand it.

You use your _____ to smell.

Smell tells you how things _____.

You use your _____ to taste.

Taste tells you if food is sweet, sour, salty, or _____.

Chocolate tastes _____. Lemons taste _____.

You use your _____ and skin to feel.

Touch tells you if things are _____, rough, hot, or cold.

A teddy bear _____ smooth. A _____ feels hot.

18

The Little Red Hen

A Write the meaning of each word and phrase in Chinese.

1 once upon a time _____
2 hen _____
3 farm _____
4 live with _____
5 pig _____
6 duck _____
7 cat _____
8 work hard _____
9 never _____
10 one day _____
11 find _____
12 grain _____
13 wheat _____
14 plant _____
15 think _____
16 ask _____
17 oink _____
18 quack _____
19 meow _____
20 very well (then) _____
21 myself _____

22 cluck _____
23 grow _____
24 turn _____
25 golden color _____
26 be ready to _____
27 harvest _____
28 be harvested _____
29 cut _____
30 grind...into... _____
31 flour _____
32 ground _____
33 bake _____
34 bread _____
35 finally _____
36 come out of _____
37 oven _____
38 look _____
39 delicious _____
40 won't _____
41 all by myself _____
42 all by herself _____

B Choose the word that best completes each sentence.

grains	by herself	grew	ground

1 One day, the little red hen found some _____ of wheat in the garden.

2 During the summer, the seeds of wheat _____.

3 The little red hen _____ the wheat into flour.

4 The little red hen ate the bread all _____.

C **Listen to the passage and fill in the blanks.** 33

Once upon a time, there was a little red _____.

She lived on a _____ with a pig, a duck, and a cat.

She worked _____ every day.

But the other animals _____ helped.

One day, the little red hen _____ some grains of wheat in the garden.

"We can _____ these seeds, and they will grow," thought the hen.

So she asked,

"Who _____ help me plant this wheat?"

"Not I," oinked the _____.

"Not I," quacked the _____.

"Not I," meowed the _____.

"Very well then. I will do it _____," clucked the little red hen.

During the summer, the seeds of _____ grew.

Then, the wheat turned a _____ color.

When it was ready to be _____, the little red hen asked,

"Who will help me _____ the wheat?"

"Not I," _____ the pig.

"Not I," _____ the duck.

"Not I," _____ the cat.

"Very well then. I will do it myself," _____ the little red hen.

When she had cut the wheat, the little red hen _____,

"Who will help me _____ this wheat into flour?"

"_____ _____," oinked the pig.

20

"Not I," _____ the duck.

"Not I," _____ the cat.

"_____ _____ then. I will do it myself," clucked the little red hen.

When she had ground the wheat into _____, the little red hen asked,

"Now who will help me _____ the bread?"

"Not I," oinked _____ _____.

"Not I," quacked _____ _____.

"Not I," meowed _____ _____.

"Very well then. I _____ do it myself," clucked the little red hen.

Finally, the bread _____ _____ of the oven.

It looked and smelled _____.

The little red hen asked, "Now who will help me eat _____ _____?"

"I _____," oinked the pig.

"I will," quacked the duck.

"I will," meowed the cat.

"Oh, no, you _____," said the little red hen.

"I _____ the wheat all by myself.

I _____ the wheat all by myself.

I _____ the wheat grain into flour all by myself.

And I _____ the bread all by myself.

Now, I will _____ the bread—all by myself!"

And that is _____ she did.

The little red hen _____ the bread all by herself.

Numbers from 1 to 10

A Write the meaning of each word and phrase in Chinese.

1	look at	_____	13 come before	_____
2	birthday cake	_____	14 come after	_____
3	candle	_____	15 answer	_____
4	ten years old	_____	16 question	_____
5	use	_____	17 nose	_____
6	number	_____	18 eye	_____
7	count	_____	19 less than	_____
8	There is/are	_____	20 more than	_____
9	kitten	_____	21 finger	_____
10	from 1 to 10	_____	22 left hand	_____
11	say aloud	_____	23 right hand	_____
12	in order	_____	24 both hands	_____

B Choose the word that best completes each sentence.

> two   less   more   numbers   ten   order

1   We use _____ when we count.

2   Let's say each number aloud in _____.

3   You have _____ eyes.

4   You have _____ fingers on both hands.

5   Six is _____ than three.

6   Seven is _____ than nine.

Listen to the passage and fill in the blanks. 34

Look at the _____ cake.

How many _____ _____ on it?

One, two, three, _____, five.

Six, seven, _____, nine, ten.

There are _____ candles. Jack is ten _____ old.

We use numbers when we _____.

There is 1 _____. There are 3 _____.

Here are the numbers from 1 to _____.

Let's say each number _____ in order.

1 _____ before 2. 2 comes before _____.

2 comes _____ 1. 3 comes after _____.

Now, answer the _____.

How many _____ do you have?

One! You have _____ nose.

How many _____ do you have?

Two! You have _____ eyes.

One is _____ than two. Two is _____ than one.

How many _____ do you have on your left hand?

Five! You have five fingers _____ your left hand.

How many fingers do you have on your _____ _____?

Five! You have _____ fingers on your right hand.

How many fingers do you have on _____ _____?

Ten! You have _____ fingers on both hands.

Five is less than ten. Ten is _____ _____ five.

A Write the meaning of each word and phrase in Chinese.

1	draw	19	crayon
2	line	20	thick line
3	draw pictures	21	join together
4	let's say	22	shape
5	might	23	name
6	start with	24	circle
7	curved line	25	triangle
8	type	26	square
9	types of lines	27	rectangle
10	straight line	28	round
11	wavy line	29	be made of
12	zigzag line	30	look alike
13	spiral line	31	look different
14	thin	32	diamond
15	thick	33	star
16	sharp	34	heart
17	pencil	35	oval
18	thin line		

B Choose the word that best completes each sentence.

lines	rectangle	shapes	straight lines

1 We use _____ when we draw pictures.

2 When lines join together, they make _____ .

3 A triangle, a square, and a rectangle are made of _____ .

4 A square and a _____ look alike.

Mary is _____ a house.

Can you see the _____ like these: — | ᐯᐯᐯ ?

We use lines when we _____ pictures.

Let's say you want to draw a _____.

You might start with a _____ line like this. ⌣

There are many _____ of lines.

⌢   —   ᐯᐯᐯ   ⌇   ⊚

curved line   straight line   _____ line   zigzag line   _____ line

Lines can be thin or _____, too.

Use a sharp pencil, and you can make a _____ _____.

Use a _____, and you can make a thick line.

When lines _____ together, they make shapes. ◯ △ ▢ ▭

Can you _____ these shapes?

They are a circle, a _____, a square, and a rectangle.

A circle is _____. It is made of a curved line.

A triangle, a square, and a rectangle are _____ _____ straight lines.

A _____ and a rectangle look alike.

A _____ and a triangle look different.

Here are four _____ shapes: a diamond, a star, a heart, and an _____. ◇ ☆ ♡ ◯

What kinds of _____ can you see in the _____?

spiral line   curved line   zigzag line

Let's Beat the Drum

A **Write the meaning of each word and phrase in Chinese.**

1	music	_____	16	percussion instrument	_____
2	like to	_____	17	hit	_____
3	sing	_____	18	stick	_____
4	dance	_____	19	think of	_____
5	How about V-ing?	_____	20	tambourine	_____
6	play	_____	21	cymbals	_____
7	instrument	_____	22	castanets	_____
8	musical instrument	_____	23	percussion family	_____
9	learn about	_____	24	easy	_____
10	fun	_____	25	drumstick	_____
11	That's right.	_____	26	beat	_____
12	drum	_____	27	tap	_____
13	triangle	_____	28	shake	_____
14	xylophone	_____	29	bang	_____
15	call	_____	30	click	_____

B **Choose the word that best completes each sentence.**

click	musical instruments	percussion
stick	tambourine	tap

1 There are many _____.

2 You hit _____ instruments with your hands or a stick.

3 You beat the drum with the _____.

4 You _____ the castanets with your fingers.

5 You shake the _____ with your hands.

6 You _____ the xylophone with a stick.

Do you like _____?

Do you _____ _____ sing and dance?

How about playing an _____?

There are many _____ instruments.

Let's _____ about some fun instruments.

What are the _____ of these instruments?

That's right. They are the _____, _____, and xylophone.

We call them _____ instruments.

Percussion instruments are _____ to play.

You _____ them with your hands or a stick.

Can you _____ another percussion instrument?

Did you think of the _____?

The _____? The _____?

That's right. They are all in the percussion _____.

Let's _____ them.

The drum has a _____.

You _____ the drum with the stick.

The _____ has a stick, too.

You _____ the xylophone with the stick.

You _____ the tambourine with your hands.

You _____ the cymbals with your hands.

And you click the _____ with your fingers.